CORIN'S
Quest

TALES · OUT · OF · TIME

CORIN'S Quest

DONNA VANN

Tales out of Time

Corin's Quest
Copyright © 1996 Donna Reid Vann
amended and reprinted 2003

ISBN 1-85792-218-2

Published by Christian Focus Publications
Geanies House, Fearn, Ross-shire
IV20 1TW, Scotland, Great Britain

www.christianfocus.com
email:info@christianfocus.com

Cover design by Donna Macleod
Cover illustration by Nick Mountain, Allied Artists

Printed and bound in Great Britain by
Cox & Wyman Ltd, Reading, Berks

Especially for Roger,
my best friend and encourager

Contents

An Arrogant Knight

A trumpet blast pierced the air and voices rose in excitement.

'They're coming!'

I looked up from my armful of hay to see the first of Sir Henry's horsemen crest the hill. Hoofbeats thundered on the hard road and my heart jumped at the sound. Their horses! A year had passed since the nobles' last visit and I had forgotten how tall and sleek their mounts were.

All work ceased and everyone leaned on scythes or rakes, full of the usual remarks about our manor lord and his family.

'There's Dame Margaret in the painted carriage. See that little chest she's holding? It's the family jewels - never goes anywhere without them.'

'Humph - she has her jewels, but do we get wages?'

'Take a look at them horses!'

'There's Sir Henry on the black one.'

'He's as well-fed as ever, I reckon! Pity the poor horse what has to carry him!'

'Shh! Watch your tongue, or he'll have you locked up in the pillory!'

Sir Henry rode in the middle of the long caravan on a huge black charger. I thought the horse did pretty well, considering the size of the rider. The plump lord's three chins bounced to the rhythm of his mount.

Ahead of him a couple of dozen men rode two by two. Each wore a sword at the hip and some carried spears. Although they wore no armour, I knew that some of them were knights. I stared intently at them as they trotted past, trying to guess which. There was one man with a face as dark and seamed as a walnut, who sat on his horse with dignity. He, for sure! I had my reasons for wanting to know.

Something whacked me between the shoulder-blades.

'Hey!' I yelled, nearly falling forward under the horses.

'Boy! Keep your eyes in your head, if you know what's good for you!'

It was my father, which didn't surprise me. 'Yes, Father,' I muttered, ducking my head respectfully, but I still managed to keep my eyes turned upwards to gaze at the horsemen.

Carts laden with goods creaked by, loaded with everything the nobles would need for a stay of several weeks. I even saw some windows of real glass peeking out from their wrappings.

At the rear of the procession rode a young man and young woman on horseback. She sat side-saddle on a fine white steed, while the youth rode a chestnut charger. His shiny green tunic was so short it barely covered his bottom, but its long sleeves dragged down almost to the horse's belly. His hat looked like a basin perched on his head to catch rainwater. I could tell I wasn't the only one who wanted to laugh, but we all kept straight faces and bowed or curtseyed as they passed us.

'Who's that?' I whispered to one of the village boys.

'That!' the boy replied. 'Don't you recognise Mistress Lucy?'

Mistress Lucy! I stared after the graceful girl with long dark hair. She sat very straight with her skirts tucked neatly to one side.

Sir Henry and family moved about between his several manors, so it had been a year since I had seen her. Last year she was just a little girl, thin as a hoe handle. She was Sir Henry's only child, and everybody said she was an odd one. You'd often see her out climbing a tree, and she usually carried a book instead of her embroidery.

'And the fellow is a squire called Robert,' the boy added, 'a friend of the family, they say.'

I reckoned the squire was a few years older, about eighteen, and would probably soon be made knight.

As I watched the endless rumbling train of goods and people, I felt a familiar pang. It happened every year when the nobles arrived in their silks on their fine horses. They lived a life of luxury and ease, just because they were born to it. And just because I was born on the wrong side of the stone manor wall, I was the son of a peasant farmer, a villein. I would live all my life in this one small village, working hard on the stubborn land.

I knew that was the truth, but the older I grew, the more I refused to accept it. It was a foolish idea, but I simply didn't want to be a peasant! No, it was more impossible than that. I had a dream that began so long ago, it seemed it had always been part of me. I wanted to become a knight.

I squinted my eyes shut and saw myself decked out in gleaming metal, charging into battle on a mighty steed, saving villages and perhaps even whole countries by my bravery. I'd come back to Tenham village then; I'd even bring gifts for the ones who mocked me! Once I'd made the mistake of revealing my secret to one of the village lads. Now they all knew, and they wouldn't let me forget it. I pictured the way their mouths would hang open when I rode down the village street in full armour.

I opened my eyes. The daydream vanished. I wiped the sweat from my face. I was only a stinking peasant boy who was laughed at by the whole village because I wanted to be different, to be something God never intended.

As they rode on down the hill, the squire bent his head to say something to Mistress Lucy. His neatly waved blond hair hardly moved. I ran a hand through my own tangled dark curls and wondered why the squire's hair looked like it was painted onto his head. Mistress Lucy tossed her head and laughed, her thin pale face filling with colour.

Suddenly I loathed this squire. Maybe it was the arrogant way he sat his horse. Maybe it was because knighthood would come to him easily, as a matter of course. I didn't imagine then that Squire Robert would ever notice me and dislike me just as strongly.

Hamo's Fury

'Corin, wake up!' I could hear my sister, Amice, calling, but I didn't move.

'Get up, you useless boy!' growled a rough voice, and I felt a vicious tug at my shoulder. I struggled to my feet, nearly cracking my forehead on a beam.

'I'll see you at the hay meadow,' Father added, as he prepared to leave the cottage, 'and you'd better not be late!'

I brushed straw from my tunic and hopped down the ladder from the loft where I slept, into the one large room of our cottage. Amice was crouched by the fire in the centre of the dirt floor, slurping from a beaker of whey.

My mother handed me a cup of weak ale without a word. Her thin lips were pressed together in a way that was usual for her.

'You're always the last up!' Amice chided.

I grinned and winked at her as I gulped the ale. I'm fond of my sister even though I'm much older, thirteen years to her eight. I'm nearly a man now, though, so I don't tell her everything.

She knew I wanted to be a knight, and she was the only one who never teased me about it. But I never told her I had a plan for making it begin, at least the first small step. And today was the day!

I grabbed a hunk of bread and dashed from the cottage, chewing as I ran. The dawn light was just creeping over the thatched roofs of the houses. Maybe I wouldn't be late!

'Wait, Corin!' Amice shouted. I could hear her bare heels hitting the dirt road behind me but I ignored her and ran faster.

It was an uphill run to the hay meadow. I could see the villagers all clustered around Will, the reeve, who organised the farming. I ran up and stood panting on the edge of the group. My father glanced at me and frowned, but then he nodded slightly. So I wasn't late! That was one less beating, though he'd probably find some reason to hit me before the day was over.

The mere sight of me made him angry. I reckoned it was because God had given him only one son, not enough for a farmer. Even worse, I was too tall and thin, with no strength in my long arms. 'You're just a weakling,' my father always said. It was true, but at least I could run.

Will shouted the signal, and the haymaking began. The men lashed back and forth with their long scythes, the women raked and we children stood the stalks into haycocks to dry. The bright sun made everyone cheery, and we sang or called out jests to each other.

I was well into the rhythm of gathering the cut stalks, not thinking of anything except that this was the nicest time of year. Suddenly a voice bellowed in my ear, 'Sir Corin!'

I spun around with one fist cocked. Annoyed, I saw it was Odo, fifth son of the village blacksmith, a skinny boy with fiery red hair. He was the only person in the village with time to wander about getting into mischief.

'Oh, it's you,' I said in disgust. The boy was a pest but I dropped my raised fist. I knew from past experience that blows only made him laugh.

Of all the village boys, Odo was the worst with joking remarks about 'Sir Corin'. The other lads would have forgotten the whole thing long ago, except for him.

Odo flung himself to his knees and lifted his clasped hands. 'Oh please, noble knight,' he begged, 'take pity on a poor urchin and give us some work!'

Everyone within hearing laughed, and one boy called out, 'Yes, Sir Corin!'

I pretended not to hear. I wondered sometimes if they wouldn't tease me if I had a normal name, like John or Henry or Richard. I'd never heard of anyone else called Corin.

'Why are you asking me?' I grumbled. 'I'm not the one in charge here. If you want to help, go ahead!'

Odo bounced to his feet and gave me a cheeky grin, wriggling his pale eyebrows. I turned my back on him as rudely as I could and bent to gather the next armful.

I would gladly have traded places with this imp. I was sure I was the only one in the village who thought of things like that. 'God has ordained the proper place for every person,' the old priest always said, and everyone just went along with it.

I crushed an armful of hay angrily, smelling its sweet dusty aroma. It seemed so unfair! Why

15

couldn't God have let me be born in a castle instead? The other lads just accepted the endless dull round of ploughing, sowing, harrowing, weeding. I never understood it.

The sun rose higher, and sweat ran down my back. I slipped my arms from the sleeves of my tunic and felt the air strike my dripping skin, cooling it. Most of the men had already stripped to the waist. I tied my belt tighter and left the tunic hanging around my hips. Just then a whisper travelled up and down the line: 'The bailiff! The bailiff!' Suddenly everyone was working with twice as much energy.

Quickly I bent down, grabbing as much hay as I could in one armful. The stiff stalks scratched my bare chest. The bailiff, manager of Sir Henry's estate, was a hard man who could find fault with anything.

I watched from the corner of one eye as the bailiff rode up the hill on his sturdy grey horse. In spite of the heat he wore a full garment of brown velvet that fell to his ankles, a gold belt and a broad velvet hat with a jaunty green feather. The man was not old but his hair nearly matched the colour of his horse, except it was brighter, almost silver.

He had come to Tenham from Chester three years ago, and no one knew more than that about him. People gossiped that there was something not quite right, for he talked and dressed like a noble, but he'd just turned up one day from nowhere like a travelling pedlar.

'You there - reeve!' shouted the bailiff, whose name was Hamo. 'Come here!'

Will lumbered over, grinning a gap-toothed grin.

'Yes, master?'

'Straighten your lines!' Hamo said sharply. 'You'll miss half the crop, if you let them straggle all over the meadow like that.'

The bailiff glared down at Will, who pulled his forelock respectfully and called the order. Hamo had a way of almost closing his cold blue eyes and staring at you through the slits. With his silver hair and slit-eyed look, he always gave me the shivers.

Hamo seemed satisfied, and he turned his horse towards the manor house. I reckoned the man was going to be even more of a nuisance now that Sir Henry was here - he'd try to impress his lord with how well he ran the place.

A faint breeze stirred the air, and I trembled at its cool touch on my damp skin. I had to talk to Hamo. That was part of my plan, the first step for escaping from my life as a villein farmer. It was not usual for village lads to approach the bailiff, and I had no idea how he would react, but I told myself I was not afraid of this harsh man.

Later, at midday break, I lay in the shadow of an oak at the field's edge, wondering if this would be a good time to look for Hamo. Every spot of shade was filled with exhausted workers. I didn't take any of the warmish cheese when the basket came my way, but gladly took a swig of ale, cool from the clay jug. Feeling refreshed, I jumped to my feet and trotted off in the direction of the manor.

'Hey!' I heard Odo yelling behind me but I shook my head and ran faster down the hill.

'Corin, where are you going?' Amice was suddenly at my side, clutching my tunic in her chubby fist.

'I want to come too!' she begged, jumping up and down. 'Are you going to the river?'

'Let's!' exclaimed Odo, who had caught up with us. 'It's a perfect day for it.'

'I'm not going to the river,' I said to Amice, ignoring Odo. 'Go back and leave me alone!'

'No!' Amice stamped her foot. 'Let me come with you, or I'll tell Father!'

I sighed. I knew she would, if I didn't give in.

'All right. You can come, then.' I meant Amice, but I knew Odo would tag along. 'I'm going to talk to the bailiff,' I added. It was satisfying to see their jaws drop.

'Still want to come? Or maybe you're afraid.'

'Of course I'll come,' replied Odo with a careless grin. 'Why would I be afraid?'

I glared at him. The annoying thing was, he probably wasn't half as scared of the bailiff as I was.

'Why are you going to see Hamo?' Amice demanded. 'He's an evil man! I'm going too,' she added, crossing her arms and pouting.

'I'm going to ask him if I can work at the manor.' Their eyes bulged at that. 'You know he sometimes gets village boys to help out when Sir Henry's here, and I want to get my name in first. Come along for all I care, but stay well back and don't say a word!'

We set off down the hill, with me nearly running to keep a distance between us. I didn't want them to question me further. I was not about to tell them how desperate I was to be closer to the knights who went everywhere with Sir Henry. I wanted to learn all I could by watching them. I thought that one of them might take notice of me, take me on as pupil and teach me knightly skills.

The bailiff was standing near a copse of trees by the river, talking to a hard-faced stranger, mounted on a black horse. Hamo's horse grazed nearby.

I made a downward swoop with one hand, and Odo and Amice halted. Then I stepped forward and stood in the burning sun a few paces from the men, waiting for them to finish talking. They hadn't noticed us.

'That must be the last, though,' I heard Hamo say. 'I'll have to leave then.'

The stranger nodded and raised a hand in farewell. As he turned the bridle and spurred his horse, he saw me and gave the bailiff a meaning look. Hamo whirled around. I could feel the man's anger reach out and hit me like a fist.

'P-please master - ' I began.

'How dare you spy on me!'

I didn't stop to answer. I took to my heels and ran back towards the hay meadow with all the strength in my long legs. I heard hoofbeats gaining but managed to reach the other side of the hill and fling myself down among the villagers just before Hamo came in sight. I pulled my hood over my face, pretending to sleep. It was hot under the hood and sweat trickled down behind my ears.

Hamo's horse picked its way through the peasants lying on the ground. I kept my eyes open just enough to watch him. He had lost his hat and his face was furious under his silver hair as he searched the crowd, muttering curses. But all boys wearing rough homespun look pretty much alike, and he soon gave it up and galloped back towards the manor.

The Silver Goblet

That night I lay on my pallet of straw in the loft, mulling over the events of the day. The longest day of Midsummer was near, and it was not quite dark. If I turned my head, I could see the sleeping forms of my parents and sister on the cottage floor below.

What a relief that I had outrun Hamo! I sucked in my breath as I thought of it, smelling the onions and apples stored just behind my head. I tried to remember exactly what Hamo and the stranger had said to each other. Something about Hamo leaving. Did that mean leaving the manor, for good? No one would be sorry about that!

It seemed the bailiff had something to hide. I thought it might be fun to find out what it was. I was disappointed my plan had come to nothing, but now that I thought of it, this might be even better. It would be like playing a game, if I could somehow find out Hamo's secret and reveal it. If the bailiff was doing something he shouldn't, maybe Sir Henry would reward me! I had no thought then of just how dangerous this game might be.

I began playing a conversation in my mind:

Sir Henry: 'How can I repay you, Corin, for revealing this Hamo for the rogue he really is?'

I: 'Sire, all that I ask is that I be made a knight.'

Sir Henry: 'Done!' He unsheathes his sword –

A soft noise from the room below cut into my thoughts. I had thought everyone was asleep but I knew the sound; I'd heard it often enough before. It was my mother crying. Father had beaten her earlier that evening with his leather belt. A wife had to be whipped for disobedience, everyone knew that, but as usual this was for some small thing and because he'd drunk too much ale.

I clenched my fists in fury as the whimpering continued. When I am a knight...

A light flared up, piercing the gloom. I raised my head and peered over the loft's edge into the room below. Mother stood just beneath me, a rush-light sputtering in her hand. She was opening the wooden chest which held our few possessions.

At the sight of her face I nearly gasped out loud. Her features were twisted, as if something hurt her. I felt uneasy; it was like looking into the face of a stranger.

She reached into the chest and took out her neatly folded woollen cloak. She unwrapped it and I saw a small bundle of animal skin hidden inside. What could this be?

I held my breath and watched silently, just one eye peeping over the loft's edge, as she untied the cords and lifted something out. At first I couldn't tell what it was; it flashed like a sword as she turned it in her hands.

A silver goblet! Where would my mother have found this thing, a drinking vessel fit for nobles and princes? Our family drank from beakers of wood.

I let out my breath slowly. The blood pounded so loudly in my ears, I was sure she would hear it. Where did this costly goblet come from? And why was she clasping it now to her cheek, tears streaming down her worn face?

I lay back quietly on my bed of straw, but sleep did not come for a long, long time.

When I am a Knight...

For the next few days we waited for the haycocks to dry in the fields, but even then there was no time for rest or play. I plucked weeds from the vegetable patch in the croft behind the cottage, Mother and Amice made cheese, Father sharpened and mended his tools. Our lives plodded slowly on, with nothing to break the dullness.

But behind the high stone wall of the manor, I could hear and feel the noise and bustle of an exciting life. The only time I actually saw the nobles was when they rode through the village, the trappings of their stately horses clinking and glinting in the sun.

Mistress Lucy rode out each morning just at dawn, with her father or sometimes Squire Robert. They would trot through the village, collecting an excited bunch of children who ran alongside as far as they could. But as soon as the riders reached the last house they were off at full speed, with the children cheering them on.

I hung back, not wanting anyone to see how much I envied them. Even Sir Henry sat his horse well, although he was round as a loaf. All I could think about was that I had to learn to ride like that.

And I thought about the goblet. Was it stolen? That would make my mother a thief! I couldn't believe that, but I couldn't put it out of my mind, either. I might have asked her about it, except for the look on her face that night.

At the week's end the hay was dry enough to gather. I rode with two other boys in a piled-high haycart as it trundled down the hill to the manor farm, and my father walked beside the yoked oxen. Sir Henry's share would be unloaded first, then we would dole out portions to the villagers.

'Whoa!' shouted my father. The cart creaked to a halt by the open doors of Sir Henry's hay barn. Sir Henry's farm, or demesne, was like a village in itself, with separate huge barns for wheat and barley, and an entire yard with sheds for carpenter, blacksmith and cooper.

I slid down the hill of hay to help him unhitch the oxen.

'Look lively!' snarled someone just behind us. 'You fools are too slow.'

I didn't need to turn to know it was Hamo, the bailiff, come to make sure not a wisp of hay was wasted. I touched my forehead politely but didn't look up to the man astride the grey. My fingers were trembling and I had trouble unfastening the wooden yoke. I felt myself getting light-headed, then realised I'd been holding my breath. I let it out in a puff and glanced up to see Hamo staring down at me with his slit-eyed glare.

I tried to ignore the bailiff as I helped my father pull the cart into the barn. That look might mean nothing; Hamo often stared at people that way. Or, it might mean Hamo knew I was the lad who overheard him at the river.

The men forked the hay up into the empty lofts, while we lads piled it up at the rear, to make room for more.

The bailiff stayed outside the barn until we were done, but then he dismounted and came in, letting his cold blue eyes sweep every corner of the loft. Finally he nodded and strode off.

I sighed with relief. Hamo either didn't recognise me, or if he did, he had some reason for keeping quiet about it. I rode back to the village in the empty cart, my thoughts jolting in time with the jerking rhythm, wondering what was ahead. Was the bailiff hiding something? And how could I as a mere villein boy find out what it was?

The following day was a special one, the highlight of the summer. Everyone gathered at the fallow field, where hundreds of shaggy sheep milled about anxiously, waiting to be shorn. The noise and stench were overwhelming, but this only added to the general excitement. After a hard day of shearing there would be dancing, and already the ale-wife moved through the crowd with a jug of her best brew.

There was a special skill in holding down a nervous sheep and neatly clipping the thick curly wool. I saw my father sitting on the far side of the field, gripping a docile sheep. His face was flushed under his dark red hair and his powerful arms bulged, although the sheep wasn't struggling. Just like him, I thought, to use his muscles even when they weren't needed!

All over the field piles of dirty wool rose higher and higher, as if by magic. Sir Henry owned most of the sheep, but some of the freemen kept small herds. Their sons were busily running back and forth between shearing field and smithy, keeping the iron shears sharpened. Other children helped to stuff the clumps of greasy wool into sacks.

I offered to help one of the freemen's sons sack their wool, but the boy leered at me and scoffed, 'You might dirty your noble fingers!'

Stung, I moved away, silently cursing Odo for keeping the 'Sir Corin' idea alive. I wandered aimlessly through the throng of dogs and bleating sheep and shouting men, not daring to offer my help again. Black sheep dung covered the ground and I felt it squishing between my bare toes. I hardly gave it a thought, at the time.

I saw Amice playing with her friends, right in the centre of the excitement. Mother was standing off to one side, chatting with the ale-wife.

Suddenly I thought, the whole village is here, and our cottage stands empty! I wondered what would happen if my father noticed me missing. But I pushed the thought aside. I had to look at the goblet, and this might be my only chance.

I slipped through the crowd and hurried home. At the cottage door I stopped and looked back, but the road was deserted. Even when the shearing finished I knew my parents would stay for the dancing on the green.

Quickly I opened the wooden chest, feeling around for Mother's woollen cloak. It was at the very bottom, under other cloaks and blankets. I tugged it out and took it over to the doorway, to spread it out.

Yes, there was the leather bundle. It was tied

with scarlet cord and was made of soft deerskin, finely tanned.

My fingers were shaking; I had trouble untying the cord. The silver goblet rolled out onto the cloak, gleaming in the light from the doorway. I reached for it, but then something heavy fell from the bundle and landed on the cloak with a thud.

I could tell it was a book, even though I'd never seen one up close. I picked it up; it was about the length of my hand, but thick, and much heavier than I expected. The outside was red leather, and the edges of the pages gleamed gold. Carefully I bent apart the covers, and the book opened in my lap.

'By our Lady!' I exclaimed.

I'd never seen anything like this. On the page I'd opened to were rows of brown writing, like the furrows of a ploughed field. I knew that this writing made words, but I couldn't read them. None of the villagers could read more than a word or two, not even old Father Martin.

The sides of the pages sparkled blue and red and gold; as I stared at them, I began to see pictures I recognised, stories from the Holy Scriptures such as were painted on our church walls. There was the Lord Christ in a boat on a stormy sea, but so small and delicate that I hadn't noticed it at first.

Suddenly I realised I might spoil the book with my filthy hands. I spat on the palms and wiped them on my tunic, then pushed my fingers between the stiff pages. The whole book was full of these bright tiny pictures. Everywhere was the same neat writing, except at the very end of the book. Or maybe it was the beginning, I couldn't tell. The page was blank except for a few lines. The writing tilted sideways and was smudged and spotted with drops of ink.

For the first time in my life I was sorry I couldn't read. I'd never really thought about it before. I kept turning the pages, hoping I would suddenly begin to understand the writing, but I finally decided that wasn't going to happen, so I set the book aside and picked up the goblet. Even though it was silver it looked well-used, with plenty of dents and scratches. But there was no marking, no design to tell where it came from.

Feeling let down, I started to wrap book and goblet in the deerskin when I saw movement on the road. It was my mother! Quick as I could, I tied the scarlet cord and tucked the bundle inside the cloak. I was stuffing it back into the chest when she came through the door.

She seemed about to say something and I stood waiting. But then she just pressed her lips together and began to stir the onion stew simmering over the fire.

I closed the chest without trying to explain, but I had the feeling she might have guessed what I'd been doing. I wished I could talk to her about it. I couldn't think how to begin, though, and finally I just left the cottage without speaking.

No sooner had I reached the road when I saw Father stamping towards me, his broad face purple with anger.

'There you are!'

'Yes, Father?' I replied calmly. This made him even more angry, as I knew it would.

'You idle pup! Taking yourself off when you feel like it - I'll show you what I think about that!' He yanked at my arm.

'Ow!' I yelled.

He dragged me back into the cottage, loosening his belt with the other hand. I tensed for the coming blows. Why did he get so upset over nothing? It happened all the time, so at least I was used to it.

Suddenly Mother spoke up in a small, frightened voice. 'No, husband!'

I was stunned. I'd never known her to contradict him.

'No?' John roared, puffing like a bull. 'Wife, you know better than to cross me!'

He threw me aside and grabbed hold of her and turned her over his knee, lashing her backside with the leather belt. She whimpered with every blow. There was no way I was just going to stand by and watch that!

'Father, stop!' I burst out. 'Here, you can beat me instead!' I snatched at the belt on a back-swing and jerked it out of his hand.

'Beat you!' The veins on his forehead bulged. 'By the heavens, I will!'

He tossed my mother aside like a rag doll and plucked the belt from my hand. Then he reared back and lashed me full across the face with all his might. I staggered across the room and crashed into the wall, knocking down a cooking fork. My whole body went numb with pain. I sank to the ground and put my hand to my cheek, and it came away wet. The smell of blood was strong in my nostrils.

Father stood still for a moment, breathing hard,

staring down at me. I think the sight of my blood startled him. I glared back, trying to show him he hadn't won, forcing myself not to cry out, even though the wound stung like fire.

'Clean yourself up, and I'll see you at the green,' he said finally, in a calmer tone, tying on his belt as he left. That was his way; once his rage was poured out he forgot all about it until the next time.

But I won't forget, I thought. When I am a knight, I'll be stronger than I am now. I'll come back to repay my debt, and then he can see what it feels like!

Mother was struggling to her feet.

'Are you hurt?' I asked.

She shook her head. 'But you are - your face!'

She took a cloth, dipped it into the water jug and gently cleansed my cheek. I tried not to pull away, but the pain left me gasping.

'Hold this to it; I'll run to the carpenter's wife for a poultice.'

I sat on the floor with my back to the wall, holding the wet cloth to my cheek. I was so sick of this wretched life! Was I locked into this miserable existence forever, unable to break free and make my dream of knighthood come true?

...break free... Something flickered in the darkness of my mind, the merest glimmer of an idea. The pain lessened a bit as the thought took form and became clearer. It may sound strange, but I felt almost cheerful by the time Mother returned with the salve of herbs for my face.

Encounter at the Manor

The naked sheep were led back to pasture and the whole village gathered on the green for dancing. Two shepherds piped lively tunes while everyone skipped about, ignoring old Father Martin, who stood to one side in his ragged black cassock, frowning with disapproval.

I was in no mood for dancing and just stood there lost in thought, trying not to touch my cheek. I was no closer to finding out where the goblet came from, and the book only added to the mystery. A book like that with its painted pages belonged to a noble, and a rich one at that. What if someone found out my mother had these things? She would probably be hung as a thief! At the very least, one of her hands would be cut off. I remembered a one-handed beggar I'd seen, and shuddered to think of my mother, sitting beside the road lifting a begging bowl in her one hand.

Damp fingers clutched my arm. My heart sank. It was Muriel, the hayward's daughter. Her oily face gleamed with delight as she drew me into the ring of dancers. Father had arranged for me to marry her; he said he'd made a good bargain, since the hayward's youngest son would help him with the farming. I figured the bargain was so good because no one else would have her!

'Sooner, not later,' he had said when I asked him when the wedding would be. 'I hear you've got foolish ideas, boy. Marriage will settle you down, and no mistake. You're a villein and always will be!'

I couldn't think of anything more repulsive than waking each morning to turn and see this stoop-shouldered girl with the greasy hair. What had Father meant by 'sooner'? I was afraid to ask.

I saw a shock of red hair bouncing up and down in the crowd. Odo! As if I didn't have enough trouble. The freckled-faced boy screwed his face into what might have been a grin, and beckoned sharply to me. Anything was better than dancing with Muriel. Surely my father couldn't complain if I chose to miss the dancing.

'I have to leave now,' I told the girl.

Muriel's face fell, but she loosened her grip. I felt a twinge of guilt but managed to ignore it. I ran after Odo, who was leaving the green with long strides.

'What is it?' I asked. 'Where are you going?'

Odo's looked at me to answer and his features wrinkled with concern. 'Your face!...'

The wound still smarted in spite of the salve. I shrugged irritably. 'Never mind. I'll tell you about it sometime.'

'All right.' Odo grinned, and I was glad he didn't need explanations.

He went on, 'You know how the bailiff acted when we saw him talking to that stranger by the river?'

I nodded.

'Well, I think Master Hamo is up to something.'

'Just what I've been thinking!' I said. Maybe the fellow wasn't so bad after all. 'I'd like to find out what it is, but I'm not sure how.'

'That's easy!'

'Oh, it is, is it? Well, if you're so clever, tell me!'

'We look around the manor house, first of all. We're bound to come across something, if we keep searching for it.'

'Oh, is that all!' I exclaimed. 'So we just walk through the gate and explain to anyone who asks that we're there to make trouble for the bailiff.'

'No, you idiot! But there are ways to get in. I've done it lots of times, myself.'

'And what if we don't find anything? We don't really know what we're looking for.'

'Then we spy on the bailiff, whenever we can,' he replied, in an irritating tone of confidence. 'We may see him do something wrong.'

'Oh, that's really simple! I think he recognises me - and he'll know you by your hair, unless you hide your head in a barrel. I'm sure he'll take no notice when the two of us start following him around.'

'Well, all right, maybe that won't work - but we can at least search the manor.' Odo crossed his arms. 'So, are you with me or not?'

I thought the whole thing was the silliest idea I'd ever heard, but there was no way I could turn it down. Even if we were caught and punished, I would be closer to the life I longed for, if only for a little while.

'We've got to settle one thing first,' I said.

'What's that?'

'No more 'Sir Corin'!'

Odo shrugged. 'It was only a joke,' he protested.

'No more jokes!' I said sternly, and the boy laughed and nodded.

'Then I'm with you,' I said.

Whatever I might think of this red-haired pest, I felt my mood lift. Finally I was doing something, instead of just thinking about it! At the same time I shivered with a sense of foreboding. What business did two scruffy peasant boys have, wandering about in Sir Henry's home?

'How will we get in?' I asked.

'I'll show you!'

We crossed the drawbridge over the moat and entered the main gate of the manor. The courtyard bustled with people and I felt tingly with excitement and fear. In the centre of a clutter of sheds and small buildings rose the large stone manor house.

'You boys!' the gatekeeper called gruffly. 'What's your business here?'

'We're on our way to the kennels to sweep out,' Odo replied glibly.

The man glared at us but let us pass.

'What if he'd kept us out?' I whispered. Odo walked briskly, heading in the direction of the kennels.

'Then I'd go home and get a basket and say I was bringing loaves to bake at the bakehouse.'

I was envious; what would it be like to be free of chores, to have time even to think up things like this, much less do them? After today, it would be back to work for me, with no chance to explore the manor.

As soon as we were out of sight of the gatekeeper we changed direction and headed for the manor house.

'The best place to start is the solar,' Odo said, 'if we want to find out more about the bailiff. He's in and out of there a lot.'

'What's a solar?'

'It's Sir Henry's private apartment. I'll show you! They brought real glass for the windows, you know, and there's a fireplace.'

'You must be joking!' I retorted, slowing. 'We can't go in there!'

'I've been in it three times!' Odo boasted. 'It's safe now - Sir Henry is out hunting, and his daughter usually goes with him. Dame Margaret is bound to be in the kitchen this time of day.'

My scalp prickled. 'What about the bailiff? Where is he?'

'He'll be making sure Sir Henry gets every handful of wool from his sheep.'

I hadn't seen Hamo on the green, but what Odo said made sense. The bailiff would have to be on hand, recording the sacks of wool for Sir Henry by cutting notches on his tally sticks.

An entrance from the courtyard led directly to the solar staircase. I was sure people in the courtyard were staring after us, but I forced myself not to turn around.

We were nearly at the top of the stairs when I heard voices from inside the solar room.

'Your father wants you to marry him!' This was a woman, who spoke in a pleading tone.

'Father wants!' exclaimed a girl's voice. 'Why doesn't anyone care what I want? I don't want to marry anybody yet, certainly not that arrogant peacock!'

Dimly, I heard Odo urging me to run and feet scuffling on the stairs behind me, but I stood frozen to the spot in terror.

Just then with a swish of skirts someone dashed full-tilt down the stairs, crashing into me.

Mistress Lucy! She leaped back with a startled cry. In the light from the stairwell window I could see her clearly. Her large eyes were a deep, clear blue, and her silk gown was the same colour. Long brown hair fell loose about her shoulders, and her thin face was pale except for two red spots of anger on her cheeks.

'B-beg pardon, Mistress,' I stammered in a small voice that ended in a squeak. My legs wouldn't move; even my eyes felt stuck in their sockets.

The girl stared at me. In the face of her finery, I felt ragged and dirty. In shame, I bent my head and fixed my eyes on my bare feet. Then I gasped in horror, because there were globs of sheep dung oozing out from between my toes.

I looked up to see the corner of the girl's mouth twitch. All at once she began to giggle. In confusion I backed down the stairs. I didn't hear the footsteps behind me.

'What's this?' A sharp voice pierced my numbness.

Someone jerked me up by the back of my neck like a kitten. I could turn my head just enough to see the man's silver hair. Panic squeezed the breath out of me.

'You may let him go, Master Hamo,' Lucy said with a ring of authority. 'I asked him to do an errand for me.'

'Go, then!' said the bailiff, but his hand still clutched my neck. He looked at me more closely.

'Wait a moment,' he said. 'You were the boy I saw by the river!'

I nodded, not denying it.

The man's eyes narrowed. 'What is your name, boy?'

Just what I needed - for Hamo to know me by name and complain to my father! In a whisper I replied, 'Corin, son of John the Red.'

'Louder!'

'Corin, son of John the Red!' I fairly shouted.

There was silence for a moment.

'Corin,' Hamo repeated, staring at me intently.

Hamo's voice was suddenly different, as if he couldn't breathe. Under the silver hair, his face was pale and sweating. Maybe he'd eaten some bad meat, I thought. Sometimes nobles became ill from rotten meat. We peasants didn't have that problem, we ate meat so seldom.

The feel of the man's long-fingered hand on my neck made me very uneasy. Why didn't he just beat me and be done with it?

The bailiff seemed to shake himself out of a dream. 'Watch yourself, boy,' he hissed. 'I'll know you, from now on.'

Hamo released his grip, and I bolted. I took the stairs three at a time and burst headlong into the courtyard, nearly knocking someone down. It was the bailiff's 'boy' or helper, Wat, who glared at me as I stumbled past.

Odo was slouching at the side of a shed.

'What happened?' Odo asked, as we headed for the gate.

'The bailiff scolded me, but nothing happened - no thanks to you!'

He smiled and shrugged, and we headed back to the green. I could hear the pipes still wailing.

'Maybe there's nothing to find in the manor house, after all,' Odo said. He looked bored with the whole adventure.

I couldn't believe he would give up so quickly.

'There must be! Remember, I heard Hamo say he was planning to leave. Why would he have to leave, unless he's in some kind of trouble? Maybe he steals things from the manor and hides them somewhere.'

'Maybe,' said Odo with a shrug. 'But if he'd stolen anything, it would have been discovered missing by now.'

This brought me up short.

'Well, that's true.' I had no answer for that, but I couldn't explain the man's actions any other way. 'But what if he did steal something - where would he keep it?'

Odo walked in silence for a moment. 'I know,' he said finally, 'Hamo has a separate chamber where he sleeps, over a storage shed.'

'Good! That's a start. How will we get in?' I ignored the fact that I couldn't go off whenever I felt like it. Maybe I'd have to sneak out of the cottage at night.

'We'll think of something,' Odo replied.

'Let's think it out a bit better next time!' I said.

Odo wriggled his pale eyebrows in apology, and he looked so pitiful that I had to laugh. It occurred to me that he hadn't called me 'Sir Corin' even once that day. Maybe the fellow was improving!

As we walked along in friendly silence, I began to wonder something. Why did Mistress Lucy lie to the bailiff for me? Why would a noble, and a girl at that, bother to protect a villein boy like myself? It made no sense.

I wanted to think that over, as well as the idea I'd had after my father gashed my face open. I told Odo goodbye and turned aside to the only place where I knew I could be alone.

An Unwelcome Offer

I pushed open the heavy church door. It was quiet and cool inside the small sanctuary. I breathed deeply, taking in the smell of old stone and incense.

I walked towards the altar, gazing as I always did at the scenes from the Holy Scriptures painted on every wall. My favourite was the one of Christ as a fluffy white lamb. The lamb had a soft look in its eyes; it didn't seem to notice the spear hanging from its side and its blood dripping onto the ground. I always wondered about that, why the lamb looked like it didn't care about its own wounds.

I knelt before the altar and lifted my eyes to the wooden panel showing the Last Judgment. A herd of sheep were crowded onto the left side of the painting, surrounded by smiling angels. On the right were a bunch of worried-looking goats, with flames licking their flanks. In the centre hung the crucified Christ, his face dripping huge globs of blood.

A feeling of heaviness came over me whenever I saw that painting. People said I was a good lad - everyone except my father - but they couldn't see the hatred piled up layer upon layer in my heart. It had started years ago as anger at my father, but sometimes now I felt like a black cloud was filling my soul. No, I wasn't good!

I forced my eyes away and focused instead on the coloured statue of the Virgin Mary with child, which stood to one side. The Virgin smiled in a motherly way, just as if she wanted to hear your troubles. This wasn't the first time I had poured out my heart to her.

'You see, it's this way, Holy Mother,' I began in a whisper, 'There's a strange thing at home. Mother has a silver goblet and a book, and I don't know where she got them.'

I knelt quietly for a moment. The wooden Mary smiled encouragingly. 'I guess I'll ask Mother about it, or else try to find out on my own,' I went on. I still wasn't sure which would be best, but at least now I saw more clearly that I'd have to do one or the other.

'And there's another thing, Holy Mother. It's about Father.'

I glanced away from the painted smile and shifted my knees on the rough stone.

'The way he gets so angry - you see my face, what he did to me! I can't go on here, getting beaten for nothing! I'd rather run away.' My voice echoed faintly in the empty church. This was the idea that had come to me earlier that day.

'A year and a day, and I'd be free!' I knew it was true - a villein could go and lose himself in a town, and if his master did not find him for a year and a day, he would have his freedom.

'Then I could become a knight! No one could stop me, not Sir Henry, not my father. I know I could be a better person, if only I could get away from here.'

Carefully I searched her face for any sign of disapproval. The Virgin Mary kept on smiling. That must mean it was all right! I was certain she could have frowned if she'd wanted to. If Mary approved, she could put in a good word for me with God about the whole matter. I leaned back on my heels with relief.

A giggle - was the Holy Mother laughing at me? No, it was a human giggle, one I'd heard recently. I sprang to my feet and felt myself sweating all over like a round of cheese. Stephen, Sir Henry's chaplain, had entered the door at the rear of the church, followed by Mistress Lucy.

'Good-day, my son,' said Stephen. He was a young man with friendly brown eyes.

Mistress Lucy stared boldly at me instead of keeping her eyes meekly cast down, as I thought a noble girl should. I was sure she knew I was the boy on the solar stairs.

'Good-day Master Stephen, Mistress,' I replied, my voice squeaking like a rusty hinge. They blocked my way to the church door. I tried to edge sideways, but Stephen clapped a hand on my shoulder.

'I - I know I should not be here,' I stammered, 'but you see - '

'Never mind,' Stephen said. 'Why shouldn't you be in the Lord's house? We were just coming to look at the Bible, as part of our lesson for today.'

Stephen was teacher to Mistress Lucy; he was also the one who read during worship from the mammoth Bible. Sir Henry brought the Bible with him every year and took it with him when he left. It was kept chained to the lectern. There was no need for the church to have a Bible when Stephen was not there, since Father Martin could not read.

When the old priest chanted the Latin service in his quavery singsong, it sounded like nonsense. But when Stephen read, his voice was clear and seemed to rise and fall in the right places. Hearing Stephen, I always felt the Latin words meant something important, if only I could understand them.

'It's too bad we only have the Holy Scriptures in the Latin language,' Stephen said.

Stephen seemed to be including me in their conversation. I was afraid to leave until he was finished.

'Did you know,' Stephen went on, looking at me, 'that a great teacher named Wycliffe has put the whole Bible into our English tongue, just as we all speak it?'

I shook my head in confusion. If only I could escape! I stood on one foot and the other, while they chatted on.

'I wish we had the Bible in English,' Lucy said.

Why would a girl care about reading? I wondered vaguely. They were to cook and sew and learn how to manage a household.

'Perhaps we'll be lucky enough some day to have at least the Gospels in English,' Stephen said. 'I have a good friend in Oxford who might be able to get such a book for us.'

Suddenly the church door burst open with a bang, and a loud wail pierced the air.

'Cor-in!'

Amice! Whatever could she want? She ran in sobbing, and flung herself into my arms.

I was speechless, but Stephen pulled Amice gently away from me.

'Child!' he said. 'Calm down, and say what is the matter.'

A bedraggled yellow kitten leaped from Amice's arms. Mistress Lucy gave a little cry and scooped it up. It mewed pitifully and pawed at her silk dress with its tiny claws.

'Who did this?' Lucy demanded. A red wound circled the kitten's neck.

'It was Wat, the bailiff's boy,' sobbed Amice. 'He hung my Popsy by her neck, and was going to throw her into the moat and drown her!' Amice set up a fresh round of wailing, and Stephen hugged her gently, patting her shoulder.

'That Wat is wicked!' Mistress Lucy fumed, stamping her foot.

'Not really,' said Stephen with a sigh. 'He just has no brains. He does have a cruel streak, though. I must speak to the bailiff about him.'

'And I will take care of the kitten,' Mistress Lucy said. 'What is its name?'

'Popsy,' Amice said, gulping down her last sob. She was much calmer now, and seemed to accept Mistress Lucy's help as a matter of course.

'You may come with me,' said Mistress Lucy to Amice.

'And our lesson?' asked Stephen.

'We learned today to befriend God's innocent creatures!' Mistress Lucy replied as she led Amice to the door, cradling the shivering kitten in her arm.

At last I could escape! I turned to go, but Stephen joined me.

'You know, there's no need to pray to a statue,' he said, nodding at the painted statue of the Virgin Mary. 'It's only wood. You can speak your heart directly to the Lord Christ, whenever you want.'

I felt myself flush hot and cold. Had he overheard? What if he knew I was wanting to leave Tenham, and told Sir Henry!

'I'm starting a school for the village lads,' Stephen said, as we left the church. 'I'll be teaching some of the lads to read. You seem a likely one - how about joining us?'

'What for?' I asked.

Stephen turned his kind brown eyes on me. 'I know boys just such as you who have studied and become priests. The Black Death killed off so many, there haven't been enough for years and years.'

'Priests! Perhaps that, but not - ' I broke off quickly and walked on. 'My father needs me, since I am the only boy,' I added. Besides, I thought, I had a better plan for my life than staying in Tenham village.

'It wouldn't take the whole day,' said Stephen. 'Your name is - ?'

'Corin, son of John the Red.'

'Corin, we'll talk more of this later.' He clapped me on the shoulder and turned off where the path forked in the direction of the manor.

As I started to move on, someone blocked my path. It was Wat. People called him the bailiff's 'boy', but he really was not that young. He was short with a pudgy face covered with sores.

I stepped to one side, but Wat moved too. Finally I shoved him out of the way, hearing his wicked chuckle behind me as I walked on.

All that evening I had to endure Amice's chatter about the manor house. Mistress Lucy had her own private sleeping chamber, and a tapestry with gold threads hanging above her bed. She had real glass in her windows, and her very own fireplace. Her brush and comb were of carved ivory.

On and on Amice prattled, until I said rudely, 'If the manor is so wonderful, why don't you move there!' Amice burst into tears and snuffled that I didn't seem like her brother any more.

That night I was restless. I kept shifting around on my bag of straw, trying in vain to get to sleep. Finally I crept down from the loft and left the cottage.

I walked down to the end of the village, past the quiet houses. A light mist was falling and it soothed my hot face. By the time I turned back, I felt calmer.

As I moved along the darkened street, I heard a faint creaking sound. I stepped out of the road and leaned against the low stone wall. Something was passing by, leaving the village. What was it? I squinted, but could not it make out.

I listened carefully to the sounds: the creaking of wood turning on wood, and a muffled complicated tapping. The creaking sounded like the movement of a cart, and the tapping? Yes, that was just the noise two horses would make, if their feet were bound with cloth. Someone was driving a cart through the village.

Who could it be? What was in the cart? Why the secrecy? I told myself I'd ask around in the village tomorrow, but I forgot all about it until much later.

When I did remember, I chided myself for not telling someone sooner.

But who would I have told? And who would have bothered about what a peasant boy thought he heard on a dark road?

I climbed back into my snug space in the loft. Amice had said I wasn't myself. It was true. Ever since I had spoken aloud the idea of leaving my home and village, I'd begun to realise how staggering it was. No one I knew had ever done it. It was terrifying to think of cutting loose and living a completely different life somewhere else, where I would be a stranger to everyone. Yet underneath the fear was the feeling of something exciting, just out of reach.

As it happened, my life was about to take an unexpected turn which made leaving much more difficult.

Hard Labour

'Up with you!' The rough voice of my father pierced my sleep.

'It's not yet light,' I protested groggily.

'But time to be off. You'll work in the manor kitchen, starting today.'

The manor kitchen! I sat up, sleep dropping from me instantly. I was stunned. The manor! It was what I wanted, but now -

'The bailiff needs a few more hands, and you'll help out until harvest time,' Father went on. 'You'll get your food, and I'll work Sir Henry's land two days a week, instead of three. A good bargain, since you eat far more than your share! After harvest, we'll have you married. The bailiff says it's a good idea.'

My father stomped down the ladder. He grabbed cheese and bread from Mother and crouched by the fire, tearing at the bread with his large teeth.

Mother looked at me anxiously as I joined them by the fire. 'Take your cloak to sleep in,' she said.

I smiled to reassure her, and her lined face relaxed. My mind whirled; I didn't know if this news was good or bad, but I didn't want my mother to worry. At least I would be at the manor for a while, but then to be married - and to Muriel! No, I was determined to escape before that.

I ate quickly and then looked inside the chest for my cloak. I saw Mother's cloak at the bottom and pressed on it with one hand. I felt a large lump - the things were still there. I knew I would come back and look at them again.

It was light enough to see by the time I left the cottage. As I walked down the road with my cloak rolled under one arm, I met an old woman I had never seen before. Her white hair stood out in all directions and her loose robe had probably been fine material a long time ago, but now the colour had washed out. Her face was like a ploughed hill, large and furrowed. One of her swollen eyes drooped oddly; with the other she was staring straight at me. She spoke, and her voice was like chestnuts rattling in a pot.

'A fine day for it,' she said. 'A fine day, but a sad day, a sad day.' She nodded her head repeatedly, a knowing look on her face.

Several villagers were already up and about their tasks, and they glanced at one another.

'Come along, dame, and break your fast with us,' the carpenter's wife called out. The old woman looked around, and then shuffled off in her direction.

So the poor woman's mad, I thought. I wondered where she had come from, where she would sleep. I didn't waste much thought on it though, for today promised to be the most exciting one of my life so far.

A few moments later I stood in the manor gateway. Servants bustled to and fro, dogs barked, a bright glow lit the bakehouse shed. The castle was casting off sleep and coming to life. Men-at-arms stood watch on the south tower. I belong here now! I thought. No one can turn me away. This is where it begins, and it won't stop until I really am Sir Corin!

'Go to the kitchen and report to Cook,' my father had said. I knew the kitchen was separate from the manor house. But which building was it?

'Looking for someone?'

I jumped and turned to see a freckled grinning face. It was Odo, laughing at my nervousness.

'I'm to see Cook,' I replied, trying to sound as if I knew my way about.

'Working for Cook? So am I! I'll show you around.' The boy dashed off leaving me to dodge people and dogs as best I could.

Even at this early hour the kitchen was already in an uproar. Cook, a plump fellow with cheeks like scrubbed red apples, boomed out his orders, and kitchen boys buzzed about in a swarm. At first I couldn't figure out what they were all doing.

'Onions!' Cook shouted as soon as he saw us.

We looked at him blankly.

'Chop onions!' the man yelled impatiently, pointing to a sack of onions on a table.

We tossed our cloaks to one side and went to work. I had never peeled or chopped an onion in my life, and I don't think Odo had either, but we tried our best. We cried the whole time from the smell and cut ourselves on the sharp knives, and by the time we finished, the onions were pink with our blood. I guess Cook didn't notice, because as soon as we were finished he was yelling at us to do something else.

He set me down beside the largest spit, where three suckling pigs were skewered. I had to turn the spit and keep the fire going at the same time.

'Use those bellows for the fire!' Cook roared above the din. 'And don't jerk the handle like that! They have to roast even.'

An old archery target soaked in water stood there. I wondered what it was for, but right away I discovered it was to duck behind, to keep me from roasting my eyebrows while I turned the spit. The smell of roast pig filled the stifling air and the juices ran together in my mouth.

That first day was exciting, full of new sights and sounds and smells. But as the days wore on these all became ordinary. I wouldn't have believed it, but life at the manor settled into a routine just as dreary and dull as anything in the village. Cook bellowed us awake before dawn and we worked flat out all morning without a break. The worst thing was feeling suffocated by the stifling air, being trapped the whole time in that hot dark kitchen.

After the huge noonday meal was cleared away, Cook would throw himself down on a pallet in the corner and begin snoring in loud brays. That was the signal for us kitchen boys: our one hour of freedom had begun!

Odo and I used that hour to explore the whole manor, from kennels to stables. We didn't dare risk the solar again, though. Sometimes I caught a glimpse of Mistress Lucy, as she rode back from the hunt, and I wondered if she knew or even cared that I lived and worked in the manor.

The most exciting place inside the manor walls

was the armoury in the south tower. Unfortunately I never got more than a glimpse through the open door. I would walk past as slowly as I dared, drinking in the sight.

On fine days the room was nearly empty; the knights would be training squires in the jousting field. But if it rained, they sat around in the armoury, whittling and joking while their squires polished helmets or rolled rusty ring-mail in barrels of sand.

In spite of the hard labour, I would have enjoyed myself at the manor except for one thing. I had the eerie feeling that the bailiff was watching me. Several times I had felt the skin prickle on the back of my neck, and turned to see that silver hair and the half-closed eyes glaring at me. I told myself I must be imagining things. Hamo should have forgotten all about me by now.

But I couldn't shake the feeling. I tried to keep an eye out and stay clear of him. Hamo often came early to the kitchen for a bit of breakfast. I knew if I turned around when he was there, I'd find him staring. It was worrying, all the more because Odo and I were hoping to spy on him. Things seemed to be going backwards!

On one particular day we spent our free hour trying to see how long we could stay in the Great Hall without being noticed. We stepped in from the courtyard and stood letting our eyes get used to the dimness. Villeins were invited into the Hall for the harvest feast and at Christmas, but still we gazed in wonder for a moment. The high wooden ceiling seemed furlongs away, and a fireplace filled the centre of the far wall. Knights' shields in every colour and design hung around the walls.

On our right was a massive staircase of oak, leading to sleeping chambers in the north tower. I saw a tapestry curtain at the stair's head quiver. Someone was coming!

I jerked Odo's arm and we dived under the staircase and flattened ourselves in the farthest corner. I hoped the shadows were thick enough to hide us! I held my breath as footsteps creaked down the stairs just above our heads.

As the person reached the doorway I saw it was Dame Margaret, Sir Henry's wife. She had something in her hands, a carved ivory box that probably held her jewels. I remembered hearing she took it with her everywhere.

I shifted my weight from one foot to the other, and the stone on which I stood made a scraping noise.

'What's that?' Odo whispered. Dame Margaret had left the Hall and the room was deserted.

'Let's find out!'

We knelt and worked our fingers along the uneven edges of the large stone.

'Pull!' I said. It was heavy, but we managed to lift it out. There was an empty hole beneath it.

'Huh! Nothing,' said Odo in disappointment.

'A good hiding place, though,' I replied. 'Dame Margaret could hide her jewels here!'

Odo grinned. 'More likely, she sleeps with them under her pillow!'

'Where next?' I asked. We still had a few moments until Cook would wake.

'The jousting field?'

I nodded happily. Left to myself, I would have spent every day at the field behind the manor where knights trained the pages and squires.

As we cut across the garden behind the manor, I saw the bailiff in the far corner of the vegetable patch. He was standing with his back to us, tossing sticks onto a small fire of brushwood. I touched Odo's arm and pointed, and we broke into a run. Hamo was the last person we wanted to meet at that moment. I was so anxious to avoid being seen, I didn't stop to wonder why the bailiff was burning rubbish. We crouched beside the field and peeked over the stone fence. Several knights were drilling sword skills with three boys of my age. These were squires, I knew, who would become knights when they reached eighteen. The boys wore steel breastplates, but their swords were of wood. How babyish, I thought!

I clenched my fists as I saw Squire Robert on the chestnut horse. He wore a plain brown tunic instead of armour and carried a long wooden lance. I watched with envy as he trotted down to the far end of the course. At the nearer end stood the quintain, a pole with a target at one end of its crossbeam, and weighted bag dangling from the other.

Robert spurred the chestnut to a smooth even gallop, lance braced against his right side. At the last moment he rose in the stirrups, aimed with his lance and struck the target dead centre. With a graceful movement he dodged the swinging weight. It had to be done just right, or the weight would have hit him on the back-swing.

I sighed deeply. I could feel it: the broad heaving flanks of the horse beneath me, the rush of air on my face in the gallop, the satisfying whack! as the lance-point hit home.

I could do that! I could learn all that fellow is learning. The hope that had fired me for years blazed up within me. If I had knightly skills, it might not matter that I was born a peasant. I had thought if I worked at the manor, I'd have daily contact with the knights, that they might even offer to teach me a few skills. A foolish idea, I now knew. I was stuck in that hot kitchen day and night, except for this one stolen hour. Suddenly I was aware of someone shouting and Odo tugging at my tunic.

'You urchins don't belong here! Get back to your work!'

Robert was glaring at us from across the field, his face flushed with anger. We scampered off, Odo laughing at the adventure of it, and me grinding my teeth.

'Don't belong here, do we!' I muttered as we ran.

I'd almost forgotten my idea of leaving but it came back now with the force of a blow. I yearned suddenly for the freedom to be my own person, to go wherever I pleased. Why should nobles be treated with respect, while we villeins were scorned like rubbish? I had to get out of this place and find someone who could train me how to be a knight! I just needed to think how it would work.

I couldn't have known then that tomorrow would change everything for me, and give me more reason than ever to leave Tenham behind.

Smashed Like a Clay Pot

Just after dawn the bailiff appeared in the kitchen, asking for bread and cheese. My hands were thrust inside a plucked goose, scraping out the innards for a sauce. I held my breath, not looking around, willing with all my might for Hamo to leave.

Phew! I let out a sigh of relief and turned, to see the bailiff standing just behind me, his eyes the merest slits.

'Cook!' Hamo called. 'I need this boy a moment.'

Cook shrugged and waved a ladle.

Hamo grabbed my ear and pulled, and I pulled back, because my hands were stuck inside the goose. I finally jerked free, wiping the goo on my tunic as Hamo led me into the courtyard.

The bailiff's glare changed into a sly grin when he saw the fear in my face. I realised I had made a huge mistake in thinking I could outwit this man.

'Stealing.' His tone gave the word the ring of doom. 'Stealing. You know what happens to boys who steal?'

'I didn't steal anything,' I muttered, staring down at my feet. The bailiff grasped my chin and wrenched it upward, so that I was forced to look into the narrow blue eyes.

'Oh, but you want to. I know your sort, and I'm watching you. You know what happens to boys who steal?'

I shook my head.

The bailiff clutched his hands around my throat. He squeezed his hands together and pulled upwards until I began to gag. Then he let his hands drop and chuckled.

'Go back to your work!' he ordered. I didn't wait to be told twice, but took to my heels.

I hadn't stolen anything. Still, I was worried. Hamo could claim I had taken something valuable, and who would believe me?

Why did Hamo single me out? The bailiff had a mammoth task, keeping the entire estate running smoothly. Why did he bother about one villein boy? I plunged my hands inside the goose and tried to puzzle it out, but I couldn't make sense of it.

To take my mind off my worries, I decided to go home that afternoon.

'Mother!' I called as I neared the cottage. 'Amice!' No one came out to greet me and I poked my head inside to find the place empty. Perhaps they had gone to fetch water, or to have some grain ground at the mill.

I was just leaving when my eye fell on the wooden chest. Life at the manor had taken all my thought lately, but now I remembered the goblet and book. I wanted to have another look at them; maybe I had missed something the first time. I would take the bundle and look at it at the manor, and put it back later. It took only a moment to retrieve the skin-wrapped parcel and tuck it into my tunic.

'Corin!' My mother stood in the doorway.

I jumped guiltily and tried to hide the bundle.

'No matter,' she said in a low voice. 'We can look at it together. It is time you knew.'

She motioned me to her side and took the parcel with slow movements, as if she feared it would burst apart in her hands. Carefully, she loosened the scarlet cords and folded back the leather flaps. Was my mother about to admit to me that she was a thief?'

We stood in the cottage doorway and stared together at the long-stemmed silver vessel and the red-bound book.

'You must never tell your father - ' she stopped and began again. 'You must never tell my husband about this.' The odd way she spoke came back to me later.

'Why, Mother!' I burst out. 'Why did you do it?'

'Why?' She nearly smiled, reading my thoughts in my face.

'You should hear what I did, before you ask why. It's a long story, but Father and Amice are helping build a new cottage for the reeve. We have time.'

I fetched two stools and we sat down outside, leaning against the cool cottage wall. It was a warm summer day, and birds played loudly in the trees.

'It was in the autumn, fourteen years ago,' she began. 'I was all alone in the west field, gathering straw for a bed.

'I saw a noblewoman and her servant, riding along the road there, towards the village. The servant called out to me, and I went to them.'

Her roughened hand stroked the book in her

lap as she talked. The hair on the back of my neck stood on end. I had scarcely heard my mother say so many words at once in my entire life.

'When I reached the road, I could see that the noblewoman was very tired. Then I noticed that she was heavy with child, and that it would come soon. The old servant was in distress.

'I told them that the manor was only on the other side of the village, but the noblewoman seemed frightened. She said something about not going where she might be known. Of course, I said they could come to our cottage and rest.

'I put the lady on my pallet and fed her bread and broth. She drank ale from her own silver goblet. She was very weak.

'Then John came home. I could tell he was angry with me, but he didn't like to show it in front of the lady. He made signs at me to make her leave, but I pretended not to see. I couldn't just turn the poor thing out!' She shifted slightly on the hard stool, her brown eyes seeing that long-ago scene.

'Then, in the night, her time came. She had no strength to cry out. She whimpered like a kitten when the pains were on her. At last the baby was born. You were a fine-looking lad, even then...' Her voice trailed off, and she pressed her thin lips together.

I stared at her. My mind couldn't grasp it. 'What does it matter how I looked?' I asked. 'What's the rest of the story?'

Mother sighed and made no reply, but sat with shoulders hunched on the low stool. She was quiet for so long that a chill began to creep over me.

Why didn't she go on? What was lurking in the story, ready to pounce on me?

'I was barren until Amice came,' she said finally.

Barren! my mother - that meant she could not have borne me, which meant - 'That woman?' I managed to croak, and she nodded.

'Yes, that woman gave birth to you, here, in this cottage. She called you 'Corin' when we laid you in her arms. She died soon after, poor creature.'

I sat there stunned. I scarcely heard what she said next.

'The old servant was so beside herself, I think she didn't know what she was doing. She asked if she could leave you with us. All she could think about was her dead mistress. Your father - John saw the good of having a son.'

I finally thought to ask, 'What happened to - the noblewoman?' I could not think of anyone as mother, except this woman who sat next to me in her worn homespun.

'The servant wrapped her body in the fur cloak she had worn - John helped her - and left with both horses that very night. We told the village that the baby was a surprise, that I hadn't known I was with child. You were small, so I think everyone believed it.'

We sat together against the cool cottage wall, silence wrapping around us like a fog, in spite of the hot sun.

With a quick motion, I stood up. 'I have to go, Mother,' I said, aware of how she winced at the title. 'I need to think this out.'

She nodded. Then she tied up the bundle and

held it out to me. 'It's yours - take it. It belonged to your real mother. The old servant gave it to me before she left. John doesn't know about the things. He would have sold them if he'd found them. For years he's feared you would run away, if you knew the truth.'

I tucked the deerskin packet into the fold of my tunic, then turned and stumbled off without a word. My steps took me away from village on the road towards Ludlow, but I didn't notice where I was going.

My life was like a clay pot someone had just smashed with a mallet. I was not the son of John the Red, villein of Tenham village. Wasn't this a dream come true? Then why this pain in my heart?

Other questions buzzed around in my brain like confused bees. If my mother was a noblewoman, did that make me a noble? Probably not - it would depend on who my father was.

I didn't even notice the changing light, or think about my evening duties in the kitchen. I walked and walked, thinking aloud.

'I might not be the son of a villein, but who can I tell? Not Odo! This thing was too deep to talk about. 'Not Amice, either.' I grinned as I thought of how she would wail and cry, if she knew.

Then I felt another stab of pain: 'She's not really my sister!' Yet how could I think of her otherwise?

That John was not my father - that was good! But my mother... I felt a sob rising. Why did I feel so guilty, like the whole thing was my fault?

It was now completely dark. I suddenly realised I had come far, and had a long journey back, with a certain beating from Cook at the end. There didn't seem any point now in not crying. I let the tears stream down my face, as I headed back to the manor.

Caught!

At first, I kept the secret to myself. I hid the bundle in the kitchen corner under the straw where I always slept. It was not a secure place, but would do until I thought of something better.

In my heart raged a fierce battle. Oddly enough, now that I had even more reason to leave home - to find out who I really was - it seemed wrong. There was no telling what John might do to my mother if I left. I was pulled this way and that, until I felt nearly torn in half.

Two days later the village and manor were in a fever of excitement: a party of nobles from the town of Ludlow arrived to spend a fortnight. Sir Henry was a distant relative of the baron at Ludlow, and had many connections there.

'This would be the time to explore the bailiff's chamber,' Odo said as we leaned against a shed, watching lords and ladies in fine silks and velvets ride into the courtyard. Through the open gateway I could see most of the village collected outside. This was as close to Ludlow as most of them would ever be and they would talk about it for months.

'I'm not so sure,' I said.

'You're not scared of him, are you?'

'Of course not!' I protested. 'But have you

noticed how he always has his eye on me? I told you what he said about not stealing. He'd love to catch me in his chamber! He'd say I'd stolen something, even if I didn't.'

'Too bad we didn't really hear what Hamo was talking about, with that man by the river,' Odo said. 'We need to know what we're looking for. Of course, he probably thinks we heard more than we did.'

I nodded thoughtfully. That might explain why the bailiff was watching us. Although, it did seem that I was the only one being watched. In any case, we had do something about Hamo, before he did something to us!

'How about tonight,' I suggested. 'With all the newcomers, Hamo will be distracted.'

Odo grinned at the prospect of a new adventure. We both shivered a little. It would be by far the most risky thing we had done.

That evening Dame Margaret sent for Cook. He clumped off with an air of importance, since the success of the guests' stay depended on his skill. As soon as he left the kitchen we all scattered. It was nearly dusk, just dark enough for protection from curious eyes.

From the courtyard I could see that for now, there were no men-at-arms on the wide wall, although I knew they walked back and forth the whole night. The bailiff's sleeping chamber was a small room built above one of the sheds that leaned against the wall. It was set back from the lower floor, making a rim of thatch just wide enough to stand on.

'All clear!' Odo whispered.

We ducked around to the side of the shed, next to the wall. I hoisted Odo up on my shoulders to the low thatched roof. Getting myself up was harder, but with a couple of leaps and a hand from Odo, I made it.

Our bare feet made scrunching sounds on the thatch as we crept over to the uncovered window and peered in. All was dark and still. We had to turn sideways to squeeze through, but soon we were standing inside the tiny room.

I could make out a straw pallet on the floor, and a candleholder next to it. There was just enough space left for a large chest.

'If he's hiding anything,' I whispered, 'it would be in there!'

Odo flung back the lid of the carved chest and was about to thrust in his hands when I grabbed his arm.

'Careful!' I warned. 'We'd better leave everything as it was, or Hamo will know.'

One thing at a time, we took out the contents of the chest. A few articles of clothing, a belt with a sheathed dagger attached, and a woollen bedcover were all we found.

'Nothing!' Odo exclaimed. He sounded as disappointed as I felt.

We put everything back as neatly as we could, and flopped down in discouragement next to the chest. This was our last hope to find something against Hamo. I couldn't think where else to look. Maybe we were wrong about the bailiff. Maybe there was nothing to find.

I sighed. I wasn't ready to tell Odo everything, but I needed to talk over my idea with someone. Maybe if I talked about it, I could sort out what to do.

'There's something I've been wanting to tell you,' I began.

'What is it?' Odo sounded surprised. We were together constantly; how could we have any secrets?

'I'm thinking about running away.' I heard the strain in my voice.

'Running away?' In the dimness I could just see Odo push both hands through his hair until it stood on end. 'Why? Where?'

'To Ludlow.' Answering why was harder. I was in no mood to have my friend start up again with taunts of 'Sir Corin'! Finally I said, 'I want to see what real life is like.'

'Then I'll go with you! I've never been as far as the town.'

Immediately I felt better. I hadn't expected that!

'It might be dangerous,' I warned.

'So much the better!' Odo said with a wide grin. 'When, and how?'

I didn't know, but I began turning over some possibilities in my mind. I was thinking hard and not alert to any sounds, but suddenly I heard a creak from the corner where a ladder led down to the storeroom.

'He's coming!' I whispered in alarm.

Just then a head popped up through the opening in the floor, glowing eerily above a lit candle.

'Who's there? Thieves!' roared the bailiff.

He leaped into the room and grabbed the back

of my tunic. Odo tumbled through the narrow window and rolled like a ball over the roof's edge, but Hamo held onto me and thrust the candle under my chin.

'I thought as much! I warned you, boy.'

As he dragged me to the ladder the bailiff snatched up the candleholder from beside his bed, and carried it along as he tugged me through the courtyard and up the stairs into the solar.

Sir Henry sat in a carved chair with his back to the fire. The room was filled with nobles, who all stopped talking and stared. Just for an instant I saw Lucy, who gave me a look filled with pity. I bent my head in shame. It was the same look she'd given Amice's wounded cat!

'What's this?' asked Sir Henry in an annoyed tone.

'This boy, Sire- I caught him in my chamber, stealing!'

'Stealing what, bailiff? I don't pay you that well!' The nobles chuckled and Sir Henry grinned at his little joke.

'This candlestick, Sire.' Hamo held the object aloft. It was an ordinary metal holder with a stub of candle. Some of the nobles laughed. Sir Henry frowned impatiently.

'Who is the boy?' he asked.

'One of your kitchen boys, Sire.'

Sir Henry patted his round belly thoughtfully.

'Boy!' he said. 'What were you doing, just looking for a bit of excitement?'

I managed to raise my head enough to look Sir Henry in the eye.

'Yes, Sire,' I replied, hating the meek, scared sound in my voice.

'Let him go, bailiff. He won't do it again. Right now it's as much as my life is worth to annoy Cook!'

Everyone laughed and Henry took up his conversation again.

The bailiff's face turned scarlet under his silver hair. He jerked me around and marched outside. 'I'm not finished with you!' he said.

Once out of sight of the nobles Hamo tossed me to the ground and gave me several kicks in the ribs with his pointed boot. After he'd gone, I lay still for a few moments. It was more clear than ever that I should leave. It wasn't safe here any longer, with Hamo after me.

An Excellent Plan

The next day John the Red came to the manor looking for me. I felt tense and awkward as I greeted him. I would still call him 'Father' to his face, but not in my heart.

'Hello, Father.'

'Don't you 'hello' me,' he growled angrily.

'What did I do now?' I protested, trying to keep a childish whine out of my voice.

He grabbed my arm and called to Cook, 'I'll talk to my son, then you'll have him back.'

He dragged me across the courtyard and out the gate. As soon as we were alone, he bellowed, 'You're a peasant boy! You're not some fine soft lad what can sit around all day in a school, while there's work to be done!'

In the gush of hot words I heard 'school' and began to see.

'I told Master Stephen that I didn't want to learn to read,' I cut in. John sputtered to a stop.

'I told him,' I went on, 'that I didn't see any use for it, for a peasant boy like me.'

'Well - well, that's all right, then,' he replied, a shade less heatedly. 'He never told me that. Just went on and on about what a likely lad you were, and how I shouldn't be afraid to give you a chance to learn. Even said you might make a priest someday. A PRIEST, by our Lady! Get you married to that girl, the sooner the better!'

I was shaking with anger, and for once I didn't bother to hide it.

'I didn't want to learn to read,' I said, spitting the words in his face. 'I don't want to become a priest. But why couldn't I learn to read, if I wanted to? Maybe I do want to, after all!' I stuck out my chin and waited for a reaction.

I wasn't disappointed. John struck me a blow that made me stagger and I felt my wound split open. He was speechless with rage and the blood rushed to his face. I had never dared to argue with him so openly before. He raised his hand to strike again but all of a sudden he whirled around and ran down the village street.

I dropped to the ground beside a low stone wall and put my head in my hands. Anger welled up within me like a river in flood. I'm no better than he is, I thought miserably. I was furious with John, but also with Stephen, for going to John without even asking me. I could have told Stephen this would happen!

I didn't even have time to catch my breath before something fell on me as if out of the sky. Someone was striking me again and again with plump fists. I hit back and rolled with my attacker into the street. Then I saw it was Wat, who must have jumped down on me from the wall.

I was taller and stronger but Wat's fleshiness protected him from my blows. He landed his fat fist right on my wound, which was already bleeding, and the dirt road around us turned red.

'Halt, both of you, or I'll have you up to the bailiff!'

The reeve pushed between us with his strong arms. He looked concerned for my face.

'It's nothing.' I stanched the flow with the edge of my tunic and staggered to my feet. Wat had disappeared, and I was thankful not to see John among the few people standing nearby. In fact, almost no one was about except Odo, who must have escaped when Cook's back was turned.

'Come on, I'll help you wash up.' Odo took my arm and led me in the direction of the well on the village green.

When we got there we saw a large crowd of villagers and a man standing on the well's edge.

'You people, listen to me!' shouted the man on the well, waving a small worn book. He was lean, with an earnest face. He wore a plain russet robe tied at the waist, and his feet were bare. I guessed he was a travelling friar; I'd heard them preaching in the village before.

A little to one side a plump man sat astride a sleek donkey. His red velvet jacket was trimmed with ermine and he wore a jewelled belt and little pointed boots. He clutched a fat satchel to his side, as if he were afraid someone would steal it.

'You know that the Lord Christ was humble, a man of the people,' the lean man went on. 'But in the church you hear God's word in Latin. God never intended that! He wants you to have his Scriptures in your own language!'

A shocked gasp went up from the crowd.

'And men like this Pardoner here,' he went on,

gesturing at the plump man on the donkey, 'make themselves rich in the name of religion. This man says you can buy forgiveness for your sins from him. Blasphemy!'

He was so worked up, he nearly choked on the word. The plump man glared and hugged his purse more tightly.

'Who is the friar?' I whispered to a woman next to me.

'That's no friar,' she replied; 'it's one of those Lollards, followers of the teacher Wycliffe. They go around preaching against the church. There is some truth in what he says, though.' This last she said in a lowered tone.

'Christ alone can forgive your sins,' the Lollard shouted. 'You don't pay someone to have them forgiven. Christ himself paid the price for you, when he died on the cross. Don't be foolish! Seek the truth, and you will find it! Knock, and the door will be opened to you!'

'Fine day, fine day!' rasped a voice in my ear.

I whirled around to see the old madwoman just behind me, nodding at me with her lumpy face and droopy eye. Meg, she said her name was, and the villagers called her 'Mad Meg.' She slept where she could and wandered through the village during the day, often turning up in an open doorway at mealtime. The woman seemed harmless enough, but she had a way of rising up out of nowhere and following a person around.

'Let me through, please!'

Master Stephen shouldered his way through the crowd. The preacher broke into a huge grin.

'Stephen!'

'Thomas! All the way from Oxford!'

The two men greeted each other warmly.

'Stay the night at the manor,' Stephen said. 'Sir Henry would wish it, I'm sure.' Then Stephen noticed the Pardoner. 'And you as well, master.'

There was chuckling among the villagers as Stephen led both men through the manor gate. Someone remarked it would an interesting evening in the Great Hall!

That night I tried to find a spot on the straw that didn't make my bruises ache. I gave it up finally and resigned myself to lying awake.

So much had happened that day. As I turned it over in my mind, I wondered why John had run off. I felt good about standing up to this man who had been using me like a slave for years!

It occurred to me suddenly why John had left. Instead of beating me senseless, very likely he had run straight home and taken out his rage on my mother! I felt sick. I knew that if I'd kept my temper, John might have stayed more calm. My anger probably caused trouble for the one person I cared for! I couldn't help being angry, but it didn't make things any better.

I turned my thoughts to Wat's attack. Wat was cruel and a bit wrong in the head, but I had never seen him jump on anyone like that. I didn't do anything to bring that on, I decided. I wondered if the bailiff told him to do it? It was clear I'd better go soon, before something worse happened.

There was one thing I had to do first. It meant getting help from someone who could read. I had decided that Mistress Lucy might be willing to help me and not tell anyone afterwards. I could tell she was kind; even though she stared too much, she did look at me as if I was a real person, not a cabbage. Most nobles looked right through the villeins.

On the other hand, I squirmed at the thought of taking any more pity from her. I would just have to swallow my pride. And how would I catch a moment alone with her?

Then it came to me. Early each morning she and her father rode out of the manor, she on her white steed, Sir Henry on his black. I was sure they did not ride together the whole time, for Sir Henry would be the death of any horse he rode too fast.

I would find out which way they went and hide somewhere nearby. It was an excellent plan! I would try it out the very next morning. Odo could cover for me somehow with Cook. I felt excitement rising and tried to force myself to be calm, so I could at least get a few hours' sleep.

Wat Knows a Secret

I hid behind a willow, shivering in the morning mist. 'They ride east down the road, then turn up along the river,' a stable lad had told me. I reckoned if I waited far enough up the river, I could count on Lucy being ahead of her fat father.

I had to know what was in the red-bound book, especially the writing in the front. I thought the book may have been a gift to my mother from my father. It could give me an idea of where to start looking for my real father.

Yesterday the plan sounded right. Today it seemed completely mad: here was a kitchen urchin, sneaking off from his chores to ask the manor lord's daughter for her help!

I touched the book, tucked into my tunic. That morning before dawn I had crept into the Great Hall past the sleeping forms of servants, and hid the skin-wrapped goblet under the loose stone. It was safer there than under straw in the kitchen corner, or so I thought.

Lucy and her father might ride together the whole way, and the plan would not work. I began to hope for that. I was shaking with nervousness by the time I heard hoofbeats. One horse only! I took a deep breath and stepped from behind the tree.

The white horse shied and reared.

'Madrigal! Steady, steady....' Lucy kept her seat and soothed the horse to a halt. She glared down at me. Her cloak of deep green made her face seem even more pale than usual, except for two red spots on her cheeks.

'Why did you leap out at me like that?' she demanded crossly. 'I could have been thrown!'

I stood still as a stone, wishing I'd never taken one step out of the kitchen.

After a pause, she added 'Oh, it's the boy,' in a more normal voice. 'What are you doing here?'

'Mistress,' I began, feeling my face glowing, 'I want to ask you something.' I gulped, trying to swallow my embarrassment.

Lucy dismounted and stepped closer. 'Well, you may ask it,' she said in a puzzled tone.

'I know I shouldn't speak with you, since I'm only a villein on your father's land - '

She smiled suddenly. '"When Adam delved and Eve span, who was then a gentleman?" It's a saying Master Stephen taught me, and I think it's true!'

'What does the saying mean?' I blurted out, then felt myself blushing. Who did I think I was, making conversation with a noble?

But Lucy answered as if she talked to kitchen boys every day. 'I think it means that when God made the world, he meant for all people to be of equal importance. He never intended for one group of people to lord it over another, while the others remain forever slaves. Stephen teaches me many things like this when we read the Holy Scriptures together.'

This sounded so much like what I myself had been thinking that for a moment I was speechless. Maybe this explained why Mistress Lucy had taken my side against the bailiff when he'd found me in the solar, and why she didn't hesitate to take Amice into her bedchamber.

'Don't be afraid to say what you want,' she added.

I nodded, took a deep gulp of air, and began again. 'I have a book. It- it was given to me by my mother.' I decided to tell some of the truth and hope she didn't ask questions. 'But I can't read, and I want to know what it is.'

I reached in my tunic and drew out the book. Lucy took it from me and opened it. Her eyes sparkled and the colour rose in her face.

'It's lovely!' she exclaimed.

As she turned the gold-edged pages my thoughts soared. I rode a magnificent milky charger, swung a sword of fine steel. The crowd roared in admiration at the sight of Corin the Brave, in my tunic of spun gold, and the praise of Mistress Lucy could be heard above them all. The Black Knight would be no match for me....

Her face changed suddenly from pleasure to astonishment. She opened her mouth to say something, but she never got the chance.

'You! Boy!'

I looked round to see Squire Robert scowling at me. The chestnut horse grazed under a tree some distance away. Sir Henry was nowhere to be seen. My bad fortune that it was Robert riding out with Lucy today!

'What do you think you're doing here?' the blond squire asked sternly.

I was too startled to reply. Out of the corner of my eye I saw Lucy hide the book in the folds of her skirt.

'Come with me!' he ordered. 'And you, mistress, return to the manor, if you please.'

He seemed to expect her to obey without question. Mistress Lucy tossed her head, but mounted without a word, clucked to her horse, and trotted off.

I did not bow my head. You think I'm only a villein, but I could tell you a thing or two! I thought, sticking out my jaw.

Robert's pointed features crumpled with rage. 'We'll see what Hamo makes of you!' he exclaimed in his nasal whine.

Robert rode back to the manor with me walking ahead of him. Every so often he would poke the point of his boot into my back.

Let them do what they like! I thought. They'll soon know their mistake. My mind was in a whirl but one thing I was sure of: Mistress Lucy had wanted to make a sharp reply to Robert but did not, for the sake of keeping the book a secret.

I'd been right to trust her. I was glad I'd given her the book. I wished I could help her in return. But I was leaving Tenham, and even if I stayed, what could I do for her?

'He's a troublemaker,' the bailiff growled, after Robert told him what had happened, but I saw the pleasure in his cold blue eyes at the thought of punishing me.

Hamo dragged me roughly down the stairs into the basement beneath the manor. He unlocked a small door and threw me inside. It was dark as night and the air smelt old and stale. I heard the key grate in the lock and his footsteps going away.

For a time I lay where I had fallen. After a bit I sat up. There was a dripping sound where water seeped in from the moat. My hands rested on damp moss; at least it gave a bit of cushion, for it seemed there was no bed or even a patch of straw.

I don't know how long I sat there in the darkness. I lost all feel of the passing hours. Did this mean the end of all my hopes? What would the bailiff do with me? I tried to think what my punishment might be - dunking in the pond, being stuck in the pillory, a whipping - or something much worse. My mind was so full that I never thought to move my body, until I began to grow stiff. I groaned as I stretched my arms, which were bruised and sore from Wat's beating.

I was just dragging myself to my feet when I heard the key screech in the lock, and saw the wavering glow of a rush-light beyond the opening door. My heart surged with hope until I saw it was Wat, with bread and a mug.

'Your supper,' said Wat, grinning.

I took the food, nodded my thanks and began to wolf the bread. Wat stared at me with his evil smirk. I was too hungry to care.

'I baked the bread special for you,' Wat said finally, with a chuckle.

Suddenly I noticed the bread was different, oddly crunchy. I spat out my mouthful and looked closely at the loaf. Even in the dim light I could see it was full of small black objects.

'Beetles!' chortled Wat. His plump face creased with enjoyment.

I felt bile rise in my throat and tried to pretend it didn't matter. Wat came closer until we were almost nose to nose. I could smell his foul breath.

'I know a secret about you,' Wat said in a low, chuckling voice. 'You won't like it, if you find out. Hee-hee-hee!'

Wat began to sputter with giggles, and I wiped the boy's saliva off my face in disgust.

'The bailiff don't like you,' he added.

'I already knew that!' I retorted.

'Have a nice sleep,' Wat said. 'I'll bring your food tomorrow!' The thick door clanged shut behind him.

I spat several times. I had chewed and swallowed some of the beetles. Best not to think about it. I was dying with thirst, but there was no telling what horrible drink might be in the cup.

I sniffed it - it smelled like weak ale. For a long time I didn't drink it, but finally I raised the cup to my lips and finished it in one draught. It tasted like ale and was ale, as far as I knew, but I shuddered and flung the wooden cup to the floor.

I began to pace the stone floor with one arm stretched out until I had the feel of it: six paces each way, and I would not skin my nose on the wall.

Hunger sharpened my brain. I would walk out of Tenham the first chance I got, and look for anyone who knew my origins. I would start at the town of Ludlow, because it was nearest. Maybe I would find my real father. But even if I didn't, it would be better than staying here. And if I could keep out of sight for a year and a day, I would be free. That was the law. I could come back and flaunt my freedom under Master Hamo's nose!

What had Wat really meant, about a secret I wouldn't like? Maybe it was just something he made up, to goad me. I hoped so. It was unsettling to think that someone as warped as Wat might know a secret about me.

The rank damp smell in the cell, my hunger, the sickening beetles: all these became smaller in my mind. My plans were set. All I had to do first was to get the book back from Mistress Lucy.

Footsteps outside, and once again the key grating! Had Wat come back to harass me?

A Door Out of Reach

'Corin!'

The candlelight dazzled, so I could not see the man who stood in the doorway, but I knew his voice.

'Master Stephen!'

'I've just heard, or I would have come sooner. Are you well? Have you eaten? I've brought bread and cheese.'

I took the food gratefully and began to stuff myself while Stephen talked.

'I've spoken to the bailiff, and I'm sorry to say you have to stay in here for now, but I'll get you out tomorrow, even if I have to go to Sir Henry.'

I mumbled my thanks with a full mouth.

Stephen stood with candleholder in hand, watching me eat. He seemed to be making up his mind.

'I've watched you,' he began hesitantly, his kind brown eyes saying he meant it for good. 'You're a lad who could make something of himself. I haven't given up on the idea of teaching you.

'What do you think?' Stephen added, as I said nothing.

'You already asked my father,' I said finally, 'and you know his answer!'

I did not add that Stephen's help wouldn't be enough. I must make my own way, and couldn't even tell this kind man what I was about to do.

'Yes, I know, he seemed to be against it, but I didn't explain it very well. Perhaps if I talked to him again - '

I could only stare open-mouthed. Was Stephen so ignorant? I felt my anger rising. For all his helpfulness, Stephen didn't know much about the way things were. John would probably beat me twice as hard if Stephen said one more word.

'It doesn't matter,' I said dejectedly. 'Only please wait until after harvest.' I knew by then I would be gone.

'That's good, then!' Stephen's face lit up with pleasure, and he clapped me on the shoulder.

I blushed, feeling like a worm. I knew I would betray Stephen's friendship.

'Can I bring you something else?'

'No, thank you; nothing.'

He turned to go.

'Only - ' I began, then stopped.

'Yes, what is it?' Stephen asked, coming back to hold up the candle between us and smile his encouragement. 'I'm in no hurry.'

'It's just something I've wondered,' I said, trying to think how to say it. 'You are always so good and kind to me!'

He put his hand on my shoulder again. 'And you've wondered why.'

I nodded.

'I think it has to do with the love of Christ,' he replied. Then he waited to see if I understood.

83

I didn't, really.

'We are all Christians, yet not everyone is kind, as you are.'

Stephen grimaced at that. 'Are we all Christians? I think not. It's more than merely giving alms, attending mass, repeating words we don't understand. A true Christian is someone who has opened his heart to the Lord Christ and knows he is forgiven.'

I must have looked confused, because he added, 'That's enough preaching for one night! We can talk more of this later.' And he left, taking the candle and leaving me in pitch darkness.

Alone in the blackness that pressed in as if to smother me, I thought about Stephen's goodwill. I wasn't sure what he meant about being a true Christian, but I sensed that Stephen was different from other people.

No one else had ever bothered much about me. Villeins existed to serve the nobles; wasn't that their sole purpose in life? And even among villeins, I'd been handed mostly harshness or indifference.

Who had ever told me before that I could make something of myself? Somehow it rang true: wasn't it what I'd always believed? Why else did I think I could change from peasant to knight? An indescribable feeling stole over me as I paced the small dark cell. It was a warmth that started in the pit of my stomach and crept slowly up, until it tingled in my brain.

'You're a lad who could make something of himself.' The words pealed bell-like in my thoughts. Maybe even being a priest wouldn't be so bad, if

I could be like Stephen instead of doddering old Father Martin.

But then a sadness came over me, washing away the warmth. Whatever I could have become by staying here and working hard as Stephen's pupil, I was throwing it away by leaving. Yet how could I stay?

I stopped pacing and stood breathless as a thought struck me. Somewhere out in the wide world, if he lived, was my real father. It just might be, it was just possible, that my real father was a knight. If I could find him, I might gain the knighthood I longed for.

'I'll go and look for him!' I declared, and the stone walls echoed my words. Not even the kindness of Stephen would keep me in Tenham.

My thoughts were cut short by a familiar voice.

'Boy!' John whispered harshly through a wide crack in the door.

I put my nose to the crack.

'Yes, Father?' I felt a sharp tug on the end of my nose.

'Ow! - let go!'

'Not until we settle this! You're almost a man, and you still act like a child. The idea, trotting off to the river to talk to the Mistress! We'll see if marriage makes a man of you.'

I might have known, there was no keeping secrets in the village. John gripped my nose more tightly.

'Marriage!' I jerked free and rubbed my sore nose. 'I'm not old enough!'

'Nonsense! Your mother and I weren't older than

you when we married. The bailiff thinks it's a good idea, too. I've talked it over with him.'

'When would I marry?' I asked, panic rising.

'After harvest!'

I put my face near the crack, but kept my nose out of harm's way.

'Father, I don't feel I could possibly marry Muriel,' I protested.

'Feelings, boy! Nonsense. Get over all that soon enough. We'll both be glad of her brother's help in the fields.' John chuckled and I heard his footsteps retreating.

Marry Muriel! With everything else happening, I'd let that slip my mind. I must escape soon. The grain had ripened in the fields, and harvest was nearly upon us. Only first I would get back my book from Mistress Lucy. I couldn't leave without that.

The cell door was wrenched open next morning by the bailiff, who dragged me out.

'I'm letting you go for now,' he snarled, 'but I have plans for you.'

Hamo gripped me hard and shook me again and again in little jerks, until I was dazed and scared. Was the man mad? I couldn't believe that this was all because I overheard part of a conversation with a stranger. But what else could it be?

Hamo gave me one last shake and let me go. I stumbled to the kitchen, where Cook was on the rampage and cuffed me sharply for being gone. Soon I was back at the spit, turning it slowly as the fire flared hot.

As I crouched beside the sizzling roast pig, something made me uneasy, and I glanced over my shoulder. Wat stood grinning behind me, his piggy eyes glowing in the leaping flames.

I turned back to the fire and thought hard. It was time to take action. Whatever the bailiff was planning for me, I knew it would be something I wouldn't like.

Harvest would begin any day. I'll help with that, I decided, then be off right after, before there can be any wedding. No one would notice me missing at the harvest feast, and I might have a good several hour's start. I thought that would be the best time to go, but as so often happened, I was wrong.

The events of the last two days had left me exhausted, and that night I fell asleep as soon as my head touched the straw. Immediately I sank into a vivid dream. In the dream I was riding a horse in a thick fog. The fog pressed in so close, I couldn't see even its head. All I could see were my own tunic and hose, which were a brilliant blood-red.

Then the fog parted. We were in a dense wood, but fairly flying over the ferns and fallen tree limbs. I bent my head to the horse's silky neck and wrapped both arms tightly around it. Its coat was a milky white, the most beautiful I had ever seen. The forest was hushed except for the muffled thud of hooves hitting mossy ground.

On and on we rode. The longer we travelled the more at ease I was, until I found I was sitting tall on the bare back of the white horse, hardly holding on at all. All of a sudden a joyous laugh bubbled up from within me and spilled out. I had never laughed such a laugh in all my life.

'Hurrah!' I shouted. I felt so free, as if every

burden and weight gathered through all the years of my life had been tossed away.

Just then the white horse halted, and I saw a small wooden door set in a hillock. I could hardly look directly at it, because an incredibly bright light from behind the door was bursting through every crack and crevice.

Without being told, I knew I was meant to knock at this door. I tingled with anticipation as I bent down to knock. Whatever was on the other side, it would fulfil my deepest desires.

But I could not knock; I could not reach the little door. I looked down and saw that my hands were now chained together. And my tunic is the wrong colour, I thought. Then I fell into a dreamless sleep.

Wedding Day

The wheat harvest had begun. The bailiff sent us kitchen boys back to our homes, since every family member was needed in the fields. We had to get the lord's grain in before starting on our own, and what if the weather didn't hold?

John grumbled about this all the way up the hill that first morning. The air was cool and fresh as we walked up the hard dirt path, with the early mist wisping through the fields on either side of us. Amice hopped and skipped happily, seemingly unaware that I was tense and distracted. Mother came last, silent as usual. By unspoken agreement we had never mentioned the bundle again.

I worked that day alongside John, picking up the stalks he scythed and tying them into bundles. I never called him 'Father' in my thoughts any more, and sometimes I caught myself almost saying 'John' to his face. I was determined to keep up with his pace, and soon my arms were scratched and bleeding from grabbing the stalks so quickly. Never mind, I thought, at least I'm showing him what I'm worth! Not that he took any notice.

Towards midday I looked up to see Mistress Lucy stepping through the wheat stubble, holding up her skirt with one hand. Her other hand was gloved and on it perched a small grey hawk hooded in scarlet. A large leather pouch hung from her waist.

'Good day,' she said brightly to the workers.

We all bowed. 'Good day, Mistress,' we chorused.

Mistress Lucy walked past us towards the woodlands bordering the field. She gave me a meaning glance over her shoulder, and I knew she wanted me to follow. I bent to the rhythm of tying the sheaves, fighting down my frustration. She probably had the book with her, in the pouch! How could she think I could simply walk away from my work, with John right beside me?

I watched helplessly as she disappeared into the woods. I would just have to leave Tenham without the book. Even if it told me nothing, it would have been a good omen for my journey. But I couldn't wait any longer; I would leave the moment the harvest was done.

In spite of John's grumbling the weather held for the whole week and the wheat was finally gathered and stored in the manor barns, to be doled out after winter threshing. Odo and I were summoned back to the kitchen, to help with the mammoth feast that night. The whole village was invited, and Cook and his helpers had been working for days. Only the Christmas feast was more impressive than this. Every cauldron was bubbling, every spit turning, and the heat was like the fires of hell.

'I'm leaving tonight,' I whispered to my friend as we stood shoulder to shoulder, chopping an immense pile of plums for a pudding. 'Are you coming?'

Odo's pale eyebrows wriggled with surprise.

'Of course! I said I would. Why don't we go now?'

'Too many people about, and Cook would miss us. We'll wait until after the feast.'

'What about robbers? It's not safe at night.'

I retorted, 'It's not safe to leave our homes and hide out in a town for a year and a day! If you want to be safe, you'd better stay here.'

I was blustering, but I felt fear clenching like a fist around my heart. It would be much, much safer to forget the whole thing. But I couldn't rest until I found my real father, even if it took ten years! And I wouldn't stay here only to be chained to Muriel for life. As I'd always dreamed, I would step out of this villein world and turn my peasant self into a knight. At the thought that it really might happen I forgot my fears and grinned to myself as I attacked the plums.

I looked up from my chopping to see Amice appear at the kitchen door, wearing a long face.

'You're to come home, Corin. I'm not to say why. You come too,' she said to Odo.

We ducked out when Cook's back was turned and walked quickly down the village street. From Amice's woeful expression something terrible must have happened.

John was sitting on a stool inside the cottage, leaning against the wall. He smiled lazily when he saw us. Mother was bustling about chattering, not at all like her usual quiet self.

'It's today, boy,' John said gruffly.

'I've made you a new tunic and hose!' Mother put in. 'Here, try them on - oh, no, let's get you washed up first.' She pulled me over to a bowl of water and began scrubbing my face with a rag.

'Ow! Not so hard. What's going on?'

'Marriage, boy. Make a man out of you.' John nodded with satisfaction. 'I know you're not much for it, but you'll thank me one day, you'll see.'

'But I can't get married now!' I protested. 'I'm needed in the kitchen, the bailiff says.' This wasn't exactly true but was the first thing I could think of.

'Oh I've already talked to him. He was the one who thought of it! He said it's the best thing for you, to get married right away. Only we didn't like to tell you ahead, knowing you were so against it. Just think - the harvest feast will be your wedding supper!'

'But, Father - ' I stopped, because if he said one more word I would howl like a small child. All my careful planning and waiting, brought down by this! My hopes of leaving the village, becoming a knight - all ashes. I bit my tongue to keep myself from moaning out loud.

Mother was holding out the new tunic. She slipped it over my head and slicked down my unruly hair with trembling hands. I saw pity in her eyes, but also helplessness. I glanced around to see how Odo was taking it, but the fellow was nowhere to be seen. The thought that my friend would desert me made my spirits sink even lower.

All work had stopped in the village for the event. Freshly washed and clothed, I walked down the street with my family. On the outside I might be scrubbed and fresh, but inside I was black with gloom. At the church door waited Muriel, in a new homespun gown. Her oily face reflected the sunlight, and I could tell she was beside herself with happiness.

I darted glances around for Odo, but couldn't see the redhead. The priest would lead us in the marriage vows at the church door, in front of all the village. Then everyone would go inside for the wedding mass. I wondered if I should just try to run for it, but I knew I wouldn't get far.

Old Father Martin shuffled into the church doorway and stood next to Muriel. Soon it would be all over, my dream of a different kind of life. Once I had vowed my allegiance to this girl, in the sight of God, I could not break my vow.

Just then I saw something that made my heart jump. Odo was coming slowly down the road from the manor. In his hands were reins, and attached to the reins was a horse from the manor stables!

I held my breath and kept on walking. Odo was approaching, but slowly, so slowly!

I tensed for flight and slackened my pace as much as I could. John muttered at me and gave me a shove to make me go faster. Out of the corner of my eye I saw Odo mount the horse, and almost fall off again. The brown horse was bridled but not saddled.

Now! I sprang aside and ran as if demons were after me.

'Hey, there!'

'What's he think he's doing!'

'Don't let him go!'

John thundered after me as everyone else yelled and pointed. I threw myself astride the horse, clasped my arms around Odo, and kicked with all my might. The horse shot forward and we nearly slid off backwards, but Odo hooked his arms tightly around its neck. We stayed on!

I glanced around to see John, so enraged he couldn't run, bellowing in the middle of the street. Muriel lay sobbing in a heap in the churchyard.

We jolted down the road on the galloping horse, clinging on with all our might. The village was out of sight now, and I thought we might really make it! Before any horsemen could follow us, someone would have to first run to the manor and sound the alarm -

But only a moment later I heard hoofbeats coming up fast behind us. Two mounted men-at-arms appeared around the bend. The men galloped up beside us and one grabbed the reins from my hands, and it was over.

They led us, still on horseback, back to the village. The street was full of people; everyone who had come out for the wedding was still there, waiting to scold and jeer as we were led in disgrace to the manor. Muriel and her family had disappeared; at least I didn't have to face them yet.

John was at my side, his face red as a rooster's comb. He dragged Odo and me down from the horse. 'You! You! You!' was all he could say, and with each word he slapped me on the ear.

They led us to the manor and into the Great Hall, where Sir Henry sat in his carved armchair. All around us people were whispering that this had never happened in Tenham village before, a groom deserting a bride at the church door. I wondered if

Mistress Lucy was there, but I didn't dare look around for her.

Next to Sir Henry stood Muriel's father, the hayward, a thin little wisp of a man, and the bailiff. They glared at me as if I had just crawled out of the slimy moat.

'My son wants to say he's sorry, don't you boy!' John said, hitting me a firm blow between the shoulders.

'We don't accept the apology!' the hayward said, in a high, whining voice. 'My daughter wouldn't marry your son now, for anything! Only reason I agreed in the first place, was because she was so set on it.'

John growled in his throat and clenched his fist. I knew he would like to punch the hayward in the nose.

'Sire,' the bailiff spoke up in a low voice that chilled my soul, 'I recommend these boys be put in the pillory, as a lesson to any others who might think they sit can on a horse or run off whenever they like.'

'Yes, of course,' agreed Sir Henry. 'I'll leave that to you, bailiff.'

I wanted to shrivel up with shame. The pillory stood on the village green, a wooden frame which was clamped down over neck and wrists. We'd be stuck there, exposed to anything the village wanted to throw at us.

'Sire,' Hamo continued, 'do I have your leave to nail their ears to the boards?'

'Tut-tut, bailiff, and let the sight spoil our supper? No nailing, and remove them before the festivities.

We don't want anything to dampen the village spirits before tonight!'

I breathed a grateful sigh. This was not the first time I was glad that Sir Henry's life seemed to revolve around his stomach!

In Disgrace

Excitement filled every heart that evening except mine - and Muriel's, I guess - as the entire village gathered in the Great Hall for the traditional harvest feast.

We peasants crowded onto benches at trestle tables running the length of the room. Sir Henry and his family sat in chairs on a raised platform at the end of the Hall. Their table was draped with a linen cloth, with a large silver boat for salt in the centre. They would drink wine instead of ale, and eat fine meats not shared with us.

But no one complained. At least we would have some kind of meat for once, and the ale was good and flowed freely.

I found a space on a bench at the bottom of the Hall, as far away as I could get from my parents. John sat with his arms crossed as if made of stone and didn't join in the joking and chatting. My mother pursed her lips and kept twisting the sleeve of her tunic with her fingers.

I saw Muriel, too, her face puffy and swollen from crying. She hadn't had any friends before today, but now a group of girls surrounded her protectively, every so often darting spiteful looks at me.

I felt my cheeks burn with shame and put my head down on the wooden table. I tried my best to forget the hour spent locked in the pillory - the catcalls of 'Sir Corin,' the rotten cabbage flung in our faces, the slimy spit of the hayward. I think the man was hoping to drown me in it!

'Three cheers for Sir Henry!' someone shouted.

Others took up the chant, banging their mugs on the tables, and Sir Henry stood and bowed, impressive in a wide black surcoat worked with threads of gold. Dame Margaret sat on Henry's left, as thin and pale as her husband was plump and rosy. Her jewel case rested on the table in front of her. As all eyes turned to the front, her face creased in an anxious frown, and she put her hand over the case.

'She must think we're all about to run up there and grab her precious jewels!' exclaimed the ale-wife, and everybody chuckled.

Dame Margaret wasn't the only one at the head table who didn't look happy. Hamo sat at the end, glowering at the peasants. Several times I saw the man's slit-eyed gaze rest on me. I reckoned he was sorry I got off so lightly, and I knew he'd block my escape, if he could. I'd have to chose exactly the right moment.

'Ooh - ah! Look at that, now!' Everyone broke out in applause as a page entered the hall, carrying a large platter with a peacock which had been cooked, then covered again with its brilliant feathers. The page minced his way down the centre of the hall, minding his footing because his face was almost hidden in the peacock feathers.

Several village children sniggered at the page's

tunic, so short it barely covered his bottom. His skinny legs in tight hose stuck out like barrel staves.

Odo ducked under the table and popped out the other side, following the page and imitating his comical gait. As soon as the villagers burst out laughing, Odo bobbed under the table again and appeared in his place, looking innocent. I had to admire his cheek, especially after our disgrace in front of the whole village that day.

After supper the nobles retired to the solar, and the tables were cleared away. Four hired musicians took their places on the dais and music soon pierced the air.

I joined in the dancing, because everyone else did, and I didn't want to call attention to myself. I hopped up and down, not even trying to keep to the rhythm, my feet scrunching on scented herbs strewn on the stone floor. The herbs were wasted, because all I could smell was sweat and ale.

I caught a glimpse of the lumpy face of old Meg as I whirled past. She sat on a bench by the wall, grinning and nodding to the music, but her bulging blue eyes seemed to follow me wherever I went. I shivered and looked away.

'Ouch!' Something whacked my knee and I fell head over heels. I heard laughter and looked up to see several boys standing over me.

'Ow Sir Corin,' said one in a mock noble accent, 'oi do beg your pardon!'

'Look at the brave knight!' another piped up. 'He's too good for the likes of us - can't marry a poor peasant girl, 'cause he's waiting for a fair damsel to come along!' The others snorted rudely.

I got to my feet and hobbled off, trying to ignore them. Everyone was against me now! I slipped outside, sniffing the fresh night air. I was just wondering if I should escape now, without food or cloak or my friend, when something rustled in the shadows.

'At last!'

It was Lucy, barely visible in the twilight.

'I watched at the peep-hole in the solar until I saw you go out.'

Tongue-tied, I nodded.

She held out the book. In the near darkness I could see her eyes glowing with excitement.

'This is a very special book,' she said. 'What is its importance to you?'

I gulped, trying to swallow my awkwardness. 'I have to find the person who gave the book to - my mother.'

'That sounds exciting - like a quest!'

'What's a quest?' I asked. I had never heard the word.

'It means you are looking for something very important, and you keep on looking and looking until you find it.'

I was silent. Looking and looking and not giving up until you found it - yes, that was what I had to do.

'A quest,' I repeated. I liked the sound of it.

'But if you are on a quest, you might have to leave this place. Promise me you won't think of leaving,' Mistress Lucy urged with a quaver in her voice. 'No one understands how lonely it is, being an only child, and a girl! There's no one of my class

I can play with. I'm supposed to be meek and graceful and love handwork, and not run about. And I have to marry who they say, but I don't want to marry!... Oh, it's all so unfair!'

It occurred to me that, for all the differences in our lives we had something in common: we were both unhappy with the way things were.

'Promise?' she asked again.

'I promise,' I said gruffly, feeling intensely miserable. It was a promise I could not possibly keep, but there was no way I could explain it all to this girl. Then I remembered the book.

'But what does it say?' I asked.

'Well, first of all, it comes from Chester,' she began, but just then someone appeared in the Hall doorway.

'Mistress Lucy?'

Robert! I would recognise that arrogant tone anywhere. I clutched the book to my chest and sank back into the shadows. Lucy quickly stepped forward into the patch of light and took the squire's arm, leading him back into the Hall.

I waited a bit and then returned to the Hall, the book tucked into my tunic. I had to get rid of it; it would fall out if I danced.

I slipped under the massive staircase, lifted the loose stone, and tucked the book into the bundle with the goblet, which I'd hidden there earlier. Anyone in the Hall could have seen me, but no one was paying the slightest attention.

As I replaced the stone I glanced up at the high wall opposite, at the small peep-hole where the nobles could look down into the Great Hall from the solar. For a moment I thought I saw a face in the opening, but when I stared harder, it was gone.

Then I joined the jostling dancers, keeping on the opposite side of the room from my father. I looked everywhere for the bailiff - he was another one I wanted to avoid. But I didn't see him. Every time Odo's face whirled past, he raised his eyebrows at me as a question, but I always shook my head. Not yet - we'd leave just as the dancing was over and everyone was heading home.

Saved By Fire

At first, everything went as planned. As the musicians stopped playing, to groans of disappointment and clapping all round, we told our parents we were needed again in the kitchen, to help clean up after the feast. Even John didn't dispute that, and Odo and I slipped aside from the villagers leaving the Hall. Odo would have headed for the gate, but I put my hand on his arm.

'There's something of mine under the loose stone in the Hall,' I said. 'I have to take it with me.'

Odo raised his eyebrows quizzically, but nodded agreement.

We darted back into the Hall and under the staircase where the shadows were thickest. Servants were still about but no one noticed us.

I knelt and lifted the heavy stone, then reached in my hand and felt underneath it. It took a moment for the thought to sink in that my hand moved through air. The space was empty!

'It's gone!' I cried. How could that be, since I had placed the bundle there only a few hours earlier? To be certain, I set the stone aside, and felt in every cranny. It was hollow.

I rocked back on my heels in a daze. What would I do now? Who could have possibly taken it? Then

I remembered the peep-hole in the solar. Someone could have seen me hide the deerskin packet.

'How could it be gone?' Odo asked.

'I think someone was looking down from the solar and saw me hide the - the bundle here.' I wasn't ready yet to tell Odo what the bundle meant. 'They came and took it while we were dancing.'

'Well, it's gone now,' Odo said with a shrug. 'Let's go!'

'But I have to get it back,' I said. 'I can't go without it.'

'What on earth is it?' asked Odo. 'Did you steal something?'

'No, but - well, this thing could help us someday. I have to find it.'

'Do you think Hamo took it?' Odo asked.

'Who else?'

I thought of the night we had searched the bailiff's chest, and then sat and leaned against it as we talked. As I pictured it in my mind something didn't seem quite right.

'Wait!' I exclaimed excitedly. 'When we searched Hamo's chamber, there was something strange about his chest.'

'What do you mean?'

'Didn't it seem that the inside of the chest should have been deeper than it was?'

'Now that you say it. But what do you mean?'

'It was shallow, but the outside was larger. There must be a space beneath it! He could hide anything there. We need to get into his room and have another look.'

'We barely escaped last time!'

'I have to get that bundle,' I said stubbornly. 'I won't go until I do.'

'All right,' Odo said with a grin.

We ran over to the shed and clambered up to the roof. A quick peek though the window showed us the room was empty; Hamo was probably in the solar. A moment later we were inside and had the chest's contents laid neatly on the floor.

'Here we are!' I exclaimed.

I tried my best to slide the wooden bottom of the chest this way and that, but nothing happened. I beat on it with my fist in frustration, and suddenly one end tilted up.

'That's it!' Odo cried.

We lifted out the false bottom and felt around to see what was hidden beneath. My hands cupped over little skin bags filled with something hard which clinked as I touched it.

'Coins?' asked Odo.

I thrust my hand into one bag, and whistled in amazement. 'Where did Hamo get bags and bags of coins?'

I kept searching until I felt a different, larger bundle. I drew it out. Yes, it was mine! Hamo had taken it right from under our noses.

'Let's go!' I urged.

Odo began to replace the false bottom, when I cried 'Stop!'

Odo paused with the board in his hands. 'What is it?'

I was quiet for a moment and then blurted out, 'We should take some of the money. We may need it in Ludlow.'

Odo snorted. 'I'll bet Hamo is one to count his money every night. He'll notice right away that something's missing.'

'Just one bag, then. I'll carry it, and I'll take the danger of it.' I reached in and drew out one of the little bags. I unwrapped the book and goblet and added the coins to my hoard.

'You'll take the danger, you say, but we're in this together, and we'll be punished together,' Odo argued, his pale face just visible in the dark room.

'Then I'll say you didn't know a thing about it.'

There was something else I wanted, too. It was a slender dagger in a belted sheath, which I'd seen the first time we looked in the bailiff's chest. I took it up and unsheathed it, touching the blade gently with one finger. It was razor-sharp.

'Come on, let's go!' Odo urged. He had already replaced the contents of the chest neatly, and closed the lid.

'Wait,' I said. Pulling my tunic off over my head, I buckled the dagger belt around my waist. When I put my tunic back on the blade hung at my side underneath it, completely invisible. Then I tied my own belt as tight as possible, and placed the heavy bundle securely down my front so it rested just below my chest. It would bob up and down if I ran but hopefully not fall out.

Odo seemed uneasy. 'It's stealing!'

I shrugged. 'We'll need a weapon.' What was a little stealing on top of all my other sins: lying, betraying friends and family, running away. These all made stealing some coins or a dagger seem like nothing. For a brief moment I pictured the horrible scene of the Last Judgement over the church altar. I shook my head to clear it, and told myself I was only doing what I had to, if I was ever going to escape Tenham village.

I stood up with an impatient twitch, putting these thoughts behind me. 'I'm leaving tonight,' I said loudly. 'I warned you it might be dangerous; if you're not coming, say so now!'

What happened next was so unexpected that I didn't sort it out until later. A scuffling and someone yelling. Long fingers clasping tightly around my throat, squeezing until I gagged. Someone was dragging me to the window.

'I've been watching you, just waiting for this chance!' growled a rough voice. Hamo spat out each word fiercely. 'Too bad you had to fall out the window - but you were stealing. I told you bad things happen to boys who steal!'

We were right next to the window. The man was going to throw me out! I couldn't get air. I couldn't think. Helpless like a rabbit in a snare, I let myself be forced through the narrow opening.

'Fire!' someone squeaked. 'Fire in the manor!'

At first I couldn't think whose voice it was, or what the words meant. Then all at once I knew it was Odo. I looked across to the sleeping chambers of the manor, and saw an unusual flickering light.

My Own Flesh and Blood

The bailiff loosened his grip and I shook myself free. I hurled myself out the window and jumped from the roof into the courtyard. I rolled as I hit the ground and heard Odo plop down beside me. Without waiting to check on him I dashed across the courtyard and bounded up the massive staircase towards the sleeping rooms.

Just as I reached the top of the stairs I heard a shriek from my left. Flames were shooting up the wall in a small chamber to my right; one of the tapestries was on fire. Smoke was pouring out into the room where I stood.

'Mistress!' I shouted, then I started coughing as smoke went down my throat.

'Help us!' Lucy shrieked.

I covered my nose with the hood of my tunic and darted towards the sound of her voice. Lucy and Dame Margaret were cowering in the doorway of a chamber on the left. I grabbed Lucy's hand and hauled them back to the staircase, nearly flinging them down it headlong, and shouting 'Fire!' at the top of my lungs.

Sir Henry was running into the Hall, crying 'My wife and daughter!'

'We're all right, Father!' Lucy exclaimed, choking

back a sob. 'I was in mother's chamber, and we smelt smoke - ' She raced down the stairs and into her father's arms.

Odo must have raised the village because the courtyard swarmed with people lugging cooking pots and water jugs. We quickly formed a chain from the well to the Hall, up the stairs and into the bedchamber.

Odo and I worked shoulder to shoulder, heaving pots of water along the chain. Something fell with a crash. Everyone stopped for an instant and looked up.

'What was that?' I asked.

'That were the glass from Mistress Lucy's window!'

I turned to see Wat, his eyes glowing with delight.

'The fire were so hot, it melted the lead, and all the panes fell out!'

I glared at him. Lucy was standing a few paces away, clinging tearfully to her mother. Fortunately, she hadn't overheard. Nearby old Mad Meg shuffled from one foot to the other, looking dazed and confused at all the hubbub.

Pots and pitchers were passed steadily along the chain, until there were no more flames. The stench of burnt feathers drifted out into the courtyard.

'It's out!' someone called from the doorway, and we all cheered.

I saw the bailiff come out of the Hall and look this way and that, and I touched Odo's arm. We were just slinking away when Hamo caught sight of us.

'There you are! Sir Henry wants you.'

He hardly glanced at Odo, but his cold eyes bored straight through me. The man had just tried to kill me! If it hadn't been for the fire, I would probably by now be maimed or dead. What was it that made him hate me so much?

Suddenly I remembered two things which I had never before connected. One was Wat leering, whispering, 'I know a secret about you.' Wat, who was the person closest to the bailiff.

The other was something that happened the first time Hamo had heard my name, in the solar, when I had surprised Mistress Lucy. I saw in my mind how the man turned pale and lost breath.

I felt the life drain out of me. No! My father must be a knight, a noble and kind person. Feeling sick and despondent, I followed Hamo into the solar. I could think of only one reason why the bailiff would pay me so much mind. This evil man might be my own father! It would make sense that my mother would have been abandoned by a man like that.

As if to set a seal of truth on this awful thought, I remembered Mistress Lucy had said my book came from Chester. And the bailiff was from Chester!

If Hamo was my father, he may have known I was to be named 'Corin'. That would account for him being startled at hearing the name. I hoped with all my heart I was wrong.

Henry sat in a carved chair near the fireplace. Beside him were Dame Margaret and Lucy, looking more pale than usual.

'We have you two to thank,' said Sir Henry,

'that the fire was put out so quickly, and my wife and daughter are safe.'

'Bailiff,' he added, turning to Hamo, 'you say these two are kitchen lads?'

'Yes, Sire.'

'What are your names?'

Sir Henry was actually addressing a question to us!

'Yes, yes! Speak up!'

'Corin, son of John the Red,' I said, as firmly as I could.

'Odo, the smith's son,' piped my friend.

'Well Master Hamo, find something else for them to do. Let them work in the stables - they deserve something better than the kitchen!' Sir Henry waved a pudgy hand. My spirits plummeted. The stables! Another time I might have been pleased, but now I felt only a stinging disappointment. It would have been the perfect moment to leave - and now this!

'But Sire,' Hamo said, 'these are the boys you had put in the pillory today!' The bailiff turned red with the strain of keeping his voice polite.

'These are the same boys who tried to escape?' Sir Henry asked in surprise, looking at us more closely.

'Yes, Sire.'

Sir Henry glanced round at his wife and daughter. Dame Margaret sat as if in a daze, clutching her jewel case in her lap. He patted her arm with one pudgy hand.

'Well, bailiff,' he said, 'we can't deny they saved the lives of my family! Do as I said, and send them to the stables.'

'Yes, Sire,' replied Hamo. 'Wait for me outside,' he said to Odo and me, in what was nearly a snarl.

'What now?' muttered Odo, as we stood in the courtyard.

'We leave, that's what,' I replied as I turned towards the gate.

'Not so fast!' came a harsh voice in my ear.

Hamo plunged his hand into my hair and yanked. Tears started to my eyes. 'You're a sly one, but I know about you - more than you think,' he said in a menacing whisper, his face close to mine.

I shifted my eyes away; I couldn't look into the eyes of this vile person who might be my own flesh and blood.

A malicious laugh rose out of the darkness, and I could see the squat form of Wat, enjoying any scene where cruelty played a part.

Why would Hamo treat his own son so roughly? That was easy to answer. If the truth came out, then whatever brutal thing he had done to my noble mother would be discovered. It would be in Hamo's best interest to get rid of me or keep me as quiet as possible.

'You'd like to escape, wouldn't you,' Hamo went on.

I realised then that the man had probably overheard me say I was leaving, when we were in his chamber.

'The gate is locked now, and you wouldn't get far, even if you could get out. For now, both of you go to the stables. You'll stay there until I can think of something better.'

Hamo flung his hand forward and I went flying

to the ground. As I hit the hard dirt I felt the solid bulge of the packet hidden in the front of my tunic, and heard a small clink of coin. I lay still as death, praying the bailiff hadn't noticed.

I was fairly sure Hamo didn't know we'd discovered the hidden part of the chest, and I didn't want to give him any ideas. He strode off and Wat lumbered after him like a trained bear. But what would happen when he did notice the things missing? And even more important, when would that be? Not before we left, I hoped!

'You won't leave, will you?' asked a soft voice.

'Mistress Lucy!' I exclaimed, struggling to my feet. She must have been standing there the whole time.

'I don't feel safe with Wat about,' Lucy said. 'I think he set the fire himself! I was leaving mother's room and saw him sneaking out of my chamber. I was about to scold him when I saw the flames.'

I didn't say anything, but I agreed with her about Wat. Odo stood behind me, making little cooing sounds of embarrassment.

'Ever since I saw you on the solar stairs that day,' she went on, 'there was something about you - I guess you made me curious. I can trust you, can't I?'

I muttered something under my breath that might have been a 'yes'. I had promised her I would stay, but I knew all along I would break my promise. She would despise me for leaving, but it couldn't be helped. I had to go on with my quest, at least the quest for knighthood.

I had thought part of my quest was to find my father. But to dream and seek after a father, and find one like that!

'Oh Holy Mother,' I prayed silently, 'don't let it be true!' Just as I thought this, there came into my mind the words of Stephen: 'It's only a wooden statue.' At that I felt even more despondent than before. Where could I turn?

Later, as Odo and I settled down into the fragrant hay in a corner of the stables, we whispered our plans.

'Tomorrow - we can't wait any longer!'

'When?'

'As early as possible - as soon as no one's looking!'

Escape!

'Sad day - sad day!' the quavery voice bleated.

I jumped up, startled out of a sound sleep. Then I sighed with relief, as I saw the familiar bulk filling the doorway. Meg was about early today; the manor gates would have just been opened.

The old madwoman staggered into the stables, her white hair ghostly in the dim light. When she caught sight of me, she smiled and came closer, reaching out her wrinkled hand to pat my face. I tried not to flinch. Her touch was gentle and her fingers felt dry against my cheek. Then her face puckered into a look of worry.

'Meg knows, Meg knows!' she exclaimed in a tone of distress.

I took her arm. 'Come, it's all right,' I said, thinking the madness must come upon her more strongly at certain times. 'We'll find you a place to sleep.'

I led her to a spot in the corner where there was plenty of fresh straw. Meg heaved her bulk down, sighing gratefully.

What would it be like, I wondered, to be adrift like that, alone in the world, with no family? Then it hit me that I would be like that, before the day was out. Fear fluttered in my stomach, but I told myself I was no coward. I could take care of myself!

115

The morning was dreary and grey, with rain sure to come. We had already agreed we would simply walk out of the village empty-handed, as if on an errand. My bundle and the bag of coins were inside my tunic and the dagger hung at my side. As before, I made sure my belt was as tight as I could pull it, so nothing would fall out on our journey.

I held my breath in suspense as we left the manor gates. There was no way to know if we would meet the bailiff or not. All right so far - now we headed down the village street.

John was stalking straight towards us! I swallowed a couple of times; my mouth felt like uncombed wool.

'Hello, Father!' I greeted him.

John glared at us suspiciously.

'Sir Henry wants me to work in the stables now,' I said, aware I was speaking too loudly and cheerfully, 'because of the fire.'

'I heard. As if I didn't need you at home! And where do you think you're going now?'

I opened my mouth but nothing came out. I didn't have an excuse ready.

'Oh, the stable master has sent us to tell my mother where I am,' Odo chimed in swiftly. 'There wasn't time last night, and she'll be worried.'

'Well, be quick with it! No playing about! Show you're a good worker, and something good may come of it after all.

'There's not a father in the village would let his daughter marry you now,' John added with a sneer, as he stomped off in the opposite direction.

'Poor you!' murmured Odo when we were out of earshot.

I grinned. At least one good thing had already come of all this!

We continued on in the direction of the smithy, but passed it quickly by. Even on the road you could feel the heat from the fire inside. One of Odo's brothers was working the huge bellows at the back of the stone shed, but he didn't see us.

Finally we left the village and its fields behind. I was just beginning to relax when I heard hoofbeats on the hard road. One glance over my shoulder was enough: the bailiff! I didn't have time to wonder if it was chance, or if he knew we were escaping. I grabbed Odo's arm and we dived into the thick underbrush on the side of the road.

There was a violent rustling in the bushes next to us and we halted in panic. But it was only old Meg. How on earth did she get there? I had thought she was asleep, but she must have followed us as we left the stables.

'Come!' she urged hoarsely, beckoning with her wrinkled hand. 'Meg knows - Meg knows!'

She gripped my hand in hers and disappeared into the thickest part of the undergrowth, yanking me along. It was like being in the grip of the north wind as we tore through the thicket, brambles snagging our tunics. I couldn't believe how much strength this old woman had. It seemed like we ran for hours, until I felt ready to drop. But still the wrinkled hand clasped mine and pulled me steadily on.

Much later Meg slowed to a halt. Odo and I threw ourselves down to rest. I listened carefully but I couldn't hear anything except birds twittering. We were in the middle of a dense forest. I had no sense of direction, and I chided myself for letting Meg get us lost.

Tears came to my eyes, because of the stinging brambles. At least, I told myself that was why. I had to admit I was terrified. What if we were captured? Whatever the punishment was it would be horrible.

What would happen now? The bailiff would go back to the manor for help, I guessed. They'd be looking for us first at Ludlow, but I didn't know where else to go. Surely the town would be large enough to hide us for a while.

All the worse for me if Hamo had discovered the leather bundle missing. And his coins and dagger! It was foolish to take the bailiff's things. It would make it that much worse, if we were caught. The bundle was at least my own.

I should leave the coins behind. I reached into my tunic to get them, but then I remembered we would need food, and if we begged we would attract notice. I decided to keep the coins.

We rested for a bit, but soon Meg lumbered to her feet, wanting us to follow. Odo and I looked at each other and nodded in agreement. Might as well keep going. Her way was as good as any we could think of. The flat grey sky gave no hint of the sun's position, or we might have been guided by that. All that day we trudged through thick underbrush, until the dreary light began to dim.

'The wood is dangerous at night,' Odo said, as

we flopped down again to rest. 'There'll be robbers.'

Meg said nothing, but hummed to herself as she twisted a strand of white hair in her fingers.

I shivered. More than robbers, I feared evil spirits which might prowl the wood after dark. I was hungry, and my tongue felt shrivelled with thirst. My legs stung with scratches from the thorny undergrowth. We didn't have any provisions, but our position was hopeless any way you looked at it. A little food wouldn't change that. I was too exhausted to care. After a bit we pressed onward. The shapes of trees loomed vague and mysterious in the darkness, and I was aware of small animals rustling here and there.

'We need to find a place to sleep.' I said this bravely, but I felt shaky inside. I had heard too many tales of people who foolishly stayed in the woods at night. The tales always ended one way: 'And he was never heard from again.'

A ghostly form sailed down from a treetop with an awful cry, and something brushed my forehead.

'Yow!' I screamed, thrusting my arms up to cover my head. After a moment I laughed softly. 'Only an owl!'

Meg gave an eerie chuckle, and Odo let out his breath. I found I was trembling.

We hadn't gone far when we splashed into a shallow stream. Gratefully we fell on our knees and drank and drank. Water had never tasted so cold and fresh! I looked up with a contented sigh and noticed a glimmer of light on the other side of the brambles.

'Wait here,' I said. 'I'll see what it is.' I was less afraid now, for this was no unearthly glow, but a real fire.

I crept cautiously forward, until I saw a crackling fire. I heard laughter and men's voices and then the smell of roasting meat struck my nostrils. My mouth filled with water and I moved closer. Maybe I could steal a bite! My hunger overcame my reason, which told me these men were robbers, and dangerous.

The men had just begun to eat, and I didn't know when they would sleep. But I was hungry enough to wait it out.

Crawling back to where the others sat I whispered, 'Robbers. Stay here! If I can get food for us, I will.'

I returned to the robbers' camp and crouched on the cold ground, feeling the damp creep into my bones. Still the men laughed and talked around the dying fire, showing no signs of sleeping.

A bird peeped in the forest. I sat up with a start and rubbed my eyes. It was dawn! I had fallen asleep. I got up slowly and stretched, then peered about to see what had become of the robbers. After a moment, I realised they were still there, the sleeping forms almost invisible in the gray misty light.

My stomach was gurgling demandingly. Risking discovery, I moved slowly closer to the camp, scanning the ground for any remains of last night's meal. They should have had someone on guard, but he'd probably nodded off. Everyone was flat on the ground.

Then I saw a leather pouch tied to the trunk of a tree, well out of reach of any animal on the ground. I cut it down with the stolen dagger, and peered in. Several pieces of venison, nicely roasted! As I crept away with my booty, I could hear one or two of the men shifting position, preparing to wake. I was careful to step only where rotting leaves padded the undergrowth; the snap of a twig might have cost me my life.

Finally I saw Meg's white hair, unearthly in the coming dawn.

'Quick - we've wasted too much time!' I whispered, tossing the pouch at their feet. 'The bailiff could have travelled all night on the road and be in Ludlow by now.'

'But how will we get there?' Odo asked, his pale face wrinkled with worry.

Old Meg's broad face crinkled up in a smile. 'Meg knows- Meg knows!' she said, nodding sagely.

Again we decided to follow her lead; we had no idea of the right way ourselves. As we walked along we tore off hunks of the tasty meat and gulped them down, and I felt my spirits lift.

All that day we moved through the forest at a steady pace. Sometimes we left the trees and found ourselves following the ridge of a long hill, across ploughed fields. Once some peasants looked up from their work, startled by the strange sight we made.

Sometimes we followed the River Teme, which wound its way in and out of the forests and fields. We knelt and drank our fill whenever we could. Still, I was tired and hungry again; the meat had been eaten long ago. The energy I'd felt that morning had evaporated like the mist.

Odo kept trying to make cheery remarks but I ignored him, until he finally gave up and walked along in a wounded silence. My mind wandered in a daze. For some reason I kept picturing the judgement scene above the Tenham church altar. I shivered. I knew I wasn't good enough to be one of the sheep being taken up to heaven by the angels. God would put me with the goats, damned to a horrible, everlasting death.

I'll repent someday, I promised silently. God would honour even a deathbed change of heart, and I would be allowed into heaven. But then a little voice within me whispered, How do you know when you will die? What if there is no time to find a priest, and you die in your sins, unshriven, cut off forever? You are a thief, it whispered. You do not honour your father and mother. You get angry when you don't get your way. You've lied to those who were kindest to you.

I made my feet strike the ground harder, making shuffling sounds in the undergrowth, but I could not completely silence the little voice. I tried to remember what Master Stephen had said - something about a true Christian being a person who knew he was forgiven. Well, I was fairly sure I wasn't forgiven - so I guessed that meant I wasn't really a Christian. But then what was I? And how did a wicked person like myself change, become more than just someone who went to church and chanted the words of the service?

These thoughts made my head ache, so I turned my attention to the hope of finding my real father, who I'd thought would be a good and noble knight.

Maybe I had found him - and he was neither good nor a knight. Or I never would find him. That part of my quest seemed doomed to fail.

As I trudged glumly on, a light drizzle began to fall, gradually seeping down through the leaves above our heads. Should we even go to Ludlow? I wondered morosely.

Then I thought of my lifelong quest, which had begun long ago in my heart before I even knew a name for it. It was the longing of a village farm-boy to rise up out of his plodding peasant life and become a knight.

The silence of the forest wrapped around us like a woollen cloak. Even the birds had gone quiet. That made me think of my dream of riding through the quiet wood and knocking on the brightly lit door. By escaping, I'd opened one door; I would have to go through many doors before I reached my goal of being free and becoming a knight. And it seemed the doors were becoming smaller and harder to open.

But I would open them! I roused out of my stupor and shook my head in determination. Freedom - I could almost taste it! No longer under the thumb of any manor lord, I would live a life of adventure as Sir Corin the Brave! My fear of missing out on heaven was banished to the farthest corner of my mind. I would become a knight, and I'd do it without help from an imaginary father, a wooden statue, or anyone else! Just deciding this, I felt more clear-headed and energetic.

I quickened my pace, and at the same time the sounds in the forest came to life. A bird cawed sharply somewhere behind us and something rustled in the underbrush. If it was a wild boar, we'd have to be ready to jump for the nearest tree. I hoped we'd soon come to the end of this green prison.

Just then the forest ahead of us lightened.

'A clearing!' I exclaimed. 'Let's be careful.' I led the way to what I now saw was the edge of the forest.

'Look!' I stopped so suddenly that Odo stumbled into me.

We stood at the top of a grassy meadow, overlooking a river. On the other side of the river rose a large hill covered with row upon row of buildings, all crowded up together with no open spaces between and bounded by a high stone wall. Ludlow! The river circled the town like a silver necklace. Just below us at the town's edge rose the high walls of a turreted stone castle.

'It touches the clouds,' I whispered. So that was what a real castle looked like! It made Tenham manor seem like a peasant's hut.

'A castle that big will need extra boys in the kitchen!' Odo exclaimed, hopping up and down with excitement. 'Let's cross over there.' He pointed to what looked like the main bridge to the town, in the distance to our right.

'Too dangerous. The bailiff will ask about us there. Anybody who saw us would be sure to remember.'

Odo glanced at Meg. She had collapsed on the grass and sat quietly, twirling a lock of her hair. Her one useless eye drooped sadly.

Odo grinned. 'You're right, no one could forget seeing the three of us! Maybe we could float across on that fallen tree.'

'Good idea!'

Odo and I rolled the log down the meadow to the water's edge. Meg didn't move from her place on the grass.

'Come on!' I called, but she didn't stir.

Odo ran back and helped her to her feet, and she shuffled down the hill to the river, willing to be led but not seeming to know what was happening.

'Can we all go at once?' Odo asked.

'We'll have to. We can't go upstream, and we can't risk floating too far down, and be in sight of the bridge.'

I explained carefully to Meg what we were doing. Her bulging blue eyes stared at me solemnly, and her crumpled features were grave. I hoped she understood. If only she could hold on!

We crouched on the bank with our hands on the log, which was poised just at the river's edge. 'Hold on tight!' I reminded them, and then I shouted 'Jump!'

Odo and I pushed hard on the log and launched into the water. Meg was slower, but I managed to grab her wrist and pull her in with us. She made a heavy splash and I thought she might sink, but I yanked her arm up and she clung to the log. The sudden cold made my teeth chatter, but I hardly noticed. I was straining to see where the river would take us.

We swung around swiftly with the castle behind us; the log struck a curve in the opposite bank.

'Now!' I yelled. Odo and I let go the log and flung our arms backward to grab at the weeds along the bank. I caught a clump of grass in one hand and the shoulder of Meg's garment in the other, until she got the idea and snatched at the weeds herself.

As soon as I was out we hauled up Meg. She lay on the grassy bank, dripping and gasping for breath. We collapsed beside her, giggling with relief.

The laugh stuck in my throat when I lifted my eyes to the hill we had just left. Some men were standing on the hill, waving and shouting. I couldn't hear what they said, but even at that distance I could easily see that the tallest of them had silver hair.

A New Life Begins

'The bailiff!' I shouted, dragging Meg to her feet.

Odo and I scampered up the bank towards the castle, pulling Meg as best we could. I saw a door in the town wall, just to the right of the castle towers. Meg didn't seem to understand and we had to push and tug her along. We finally reached the door and Odo turned the latch. He jiggled it several times back and forth, but nothing happened.

'Locked!' I exclaimed in dismay.

I ran up and began pounding my fists on the wooden panels. 'Open up!' I cried. 'Please open up!' No reply. I grabbed Meg's arm and was about to run when I heard a voice muttering on the other side of the door. The lock clicked open and a wizened old man appeared in the doorway, an annoyed expression on his face.

'What is it?' he grumbled.

'We want to come in!' I exclaimed. 'Please, sir,' I added.

'You don't live here, do you?'

'Well - no,' I admitted.

'Then you have to pay!' The little man held out a gnarled palm.

In desperation I glanced over my shoulder, but the men from Tenham had disappeared.

'They've likely gone around to the bridge,' Odo said.

I nodded and turned back to the old man. We didn't have time to argue with him. 'Just a moment,' I said.

I moved off out of the man's sight and took out my leather bundle. I tried to be quick but it took some time to open it and retrieve one of the coins taken from the bailiff's chamber. I was glad I'd kept them! My tunic was dripping wet, but I reckoned the leather would protect the book and goblet.

'Here you are,' I said, handing the old man a coin which winked and sparkled in the daylight. I gasped at the sight of it. I had never taken out the coins and looked at them.

The little man's eyes went as round as the coin he held.

'A gold florin!' he whispered.

We didn't wait for him to recover and ask questions, but pushed Meg ahead of us through the doorway. At last, we were in Ludlow!

Immediately I was overwhelmed by a sense of bustle and confusion. There were so many people, on foot or horseback or riding piled-high carts, and everyone seemed to be going in a different direction. But as we walked up the steep street, I began to see there was some order to it. What I'd first taken for confusion, I now realised was simply normal life in a town.

'This is the real world!' I exclaimed. Odo was staring around with his mouth hanging open and didn't answer.

We tried to keep out of people's way and not

fall into the channel of filthy water that ran down one side of the road. Meg was leading the way again, a half-smile on her misshapen features.

I gawked up at the buildings crammed tightly side by side along the way. What could they be for? They were so tall and grand - surely they weren't mere dwellings! If they were, then every person in the town lived like a king.

On the other hand, there was a strong stench everywhere. I was used to the smells of farmyard and stable, but this made my eyes water.

I was peering upwards when someone shouted, 'Look out below!'

Before I could take in what they meant, I felt myself drenched in a mess of rotted food.

I spluttered, shaking my head to dislodge the pieces from my hair and glared upwards, but saw only a hand closing a shutter in an upstairs window. With squeals and yelps of delight several free-roaming pigs and dogs leaped onto the mess and gobbled it up in an instant.

Three well-dressed boys in the street were standing nearby, evidently with nothing better to do than laugh at me. Their faces were pink with washing and their boots looked as dainty as a girl's.

'Look at the country oaf!' one jeered. 'He doesn't have better sense than to walk under the houses!'

I darted towards them but they only laughed the harder and skipped away.

'At least we know now to keep to the middle!' Odo exclaimed.

I grinned and nodded. There was a lot to learn

in the town. 'We'd better ask someone the best way to present ourselves at the castle.'

'And quickly,' Odo agreed.

I looked over my shoulder, half expecting to see Hamo in the throng of people crowding the streets. I didn't, but we couldn't expect to keep out of his way forever.

How would I start to look for my father? I couldn't just walk the streets of Ludlow, asking likely-looking men if they'd lost a wife thirteen years before. Well, I'd worry about that later.

I scanned the crowds for a friendly face, and finally found one, a man standing on the street corner. He seemed to be selling something. Maybe he would help us.

'Ho there, lad!' the man called cheerily.

I stopped, thinking how to phrase my question. Odo ran ahead and grabbed Meg, who was disappearing down an alleyway.

'Need your hair cut?' the man asked. 'Or a tooth pulled?' He waved a bloody pliers in front of my nose, grinning to show off the gaps in his own mouth.

I drew back in horror. Then I saw he wore a belt of thick rope, into which were stuck scores of grisly teeth.

The man pressed his face closer. 'Are you ill?' he asked with concern. 'I can also let blood; cure whatever you've got!' He held up a small bowl which showed traces of red liquid.

'No - no thank you!' I exclaimed.

'What do we do now?' Odo asked as we pushed on through the milling throng.

'Meg knows,' Meg spoke up, nodding all the time. 'Fine day - fine day!'

An idea struck me. 'Have you lived here?' I asked.

Meg nodded, her face wrinkling up in a ghastly smile. 'Meg knows!'

We soon found ourselves in a small wooden shed off of a back alley, with a deformed old crone scuttering around us, offering cheese and beakers of ale. This old lady was as strange-looking as Meg, with hunched back and a nose like a broken bird's wing, but at least she had her wits. She let us know by signs behind Meg's back that she knew Meg was mad, and that she would look after her.

'Are ye hiding from someone?' she asked.

I nodded.

'Sheriff after ye?'

My shoulders drooped. I hadn't thought of this, but it was almost certain that Hamo would call on the sheriff of Ludlow to help look for two escaped villeins.

'I thought so!' she cackled, pleased with herself. She paced around us like a hound on a trail, glancing now and again at Odo. 'We'll fix that hair for you, that's what we'll do!'

Some time later I was staring in astonishment at a very fidgety Odo, his face as pale as a bowl of milk, under a shock of walnut-coloured hair.

I burst out laughing and Odo looked pained.

'Sorry - it's just that your own mother wouldn't recognise you!'

'What do we do now?' Odo asked.

'I'll take you to the castle, and have a word with the porter,' the old hag said. 'He owes me a favour, and if you two can pull your weight in the kitchen, as you say - '

As we were leaving, Meg, her bulk spread out on the straw-covered floor, nodded and smiled her crooked smile. 'Fine day - sad day!' she murmured. I told her goodbye but I don't think she noticed.

The castle will be the safest place for us, I thought. We trudged up the dirt streets, darting glances this way and that for any sign of the bailiff.

'Cook needs a few extra hands just now,' said the porter at the outer castle gates, 'as there's many come to stay for the tournament. If these two are as sharp as you say, they'll find good work here, and plenty of vittles, too!'

A tournament! An idea crossed my mind. No, it was too ridiculous. I put the thought aside, at least for now.

'You there, Nat!' shouted the porter, to a boy lounging nearby. 'Take these two to the kitchen.'

Nat sauntered carelessly across the outer bailey and over the drawbridge. The moat was waterless but very deep. As we walked beneath the huge arched gateway into the castle itself, I had the feeling I was walking into the jaws of a fierce monster. The castle didn't seem like such a safe place after all. Now my new life should begin, but I couldn't shake the feeling that all might not turn out as I hoped.

With a Leg of Pork

As soon as we came through the door of the kitchen, I relaxed. Here was the same familiar scene of shouting cook and scurrying lads, blazing spit and the sharp scents of cooking. The only difference between this and Tenham manor was that here the kitchen was much larger, and Cook a thin fellow with a sad face.

'Can you chop an eel proper?' was all he asked, and when we both nodded, set us to chopping eel for pies. Many times in the days to come, as I chopped and peeled and stirred, I pondered the fact that I had made part of my dream come true: I had escaped! I was living in a real town, and no one had caught me yet.

But was this what it was all for? More endless dull chores! I wouldn't be content to stay here very long, only until I thought the bailiff would get tired of looking for me in Ludlow town. There was no way to know when that would be. My mind was already planning ahead. I would ask for news of my father in Ludlow, and then head for Chester.

Although we worked and slept hard at the end of an exhausting day, still we found a few free moments. Odo would have liked to explore the enormous castle, but I refused. I didn't want to risk attracting notice.

I was only interested in one place, the armoury in the inner court. I walked back and forth in front of the doorway so often, I was probably wearing a path in the dirt.

Knights were going in and out of the armoury constantly, each attended by his own squire. A tournament would soon take place in the outer bailey of the castle; each new day brought a few more knights, who pitched their colourful tents just inside the castle walls. These knights were more grand in dress and manner than any I had seen at Tenham.

Even the squires were objects of my envy. If only one of them would die unexpectedly! The knight would cast his eye about the courtyard, looking for a replacement....

There! You, boy - you look like a likely fellow! I've lost a squire, but you may do to take his place. Come, let's see what you know!

I would show him I could handle a sword, I mused, as I stirred a huge wooden paddle in a pot of simmering sauce. I had watched so much training in sword skills at Tenham, I was sure I could do it myself. And I could sit a horse - maybe I'd still need some practice, but at least I wouldn't fall off.

Lost in my reverie, I slowed my circular motion. I noticed a scorching smell, and at the same moment a blow on the ear knocked me sideways.

'My sauce - you've ruined it!' The long-faced Cook grabbed the paddle and began to stir, alternately moaning and yelling at me.

I ran to fetch an empty pot. 'Look - we'll pour the top part in here; it's only the bottom is ruined.'

Cook fumed and muttered, but he helped me tip the heavy pot so the brown sauce ran into the one I had brought. Then I lifted it onto the hook over the fire and began to stir as if I would never stop.

'Not so violent!' warned Cook, but after a moment he seemed satisfied, and left me to it.

The shiny brown sauce reminded me of a horse's silky coat. I'd like to have a horse like that! I thought. This made me think again of the silly idea that came to me when I first heard of the tournament. It was absolutely ridiculous: I could never get away with it! But if I did succeed, it might help make my dream come true.

It would mean getting inside the castle armoury, of course. That wouldn't be easy; there was no chance of it ever being empty. On the other hand, it was such a large place with so much activity, that I thought I could at least walk in and out, if I could think of a plan.

Finally I thought of something that might work. At least it would get me inside to have a look. I remembered my resolution not to be noticed, but now I changed my mind. For my plan to work, I would be attracting the attention of every person at the tournament!

Next morning I stole a leg of roast pork and hid it under my pallet of straw. That afternoon, when we were free, I told Odo what I had in mind.

'But you can't come,' I said. 'Two of us just wouldn't be believed.

Odo's face fell. 'All right. But I want to try it next!'

I shrugged. I knew this would only work once.

I found a bit of clean cloth, and wrapped the pork in it. I washed my face and hands and smoothed down my hair as best I could. Then I strode towards the armoury with purpose in my step, holding the pork leg out in front of me. No-one would mistake a boy in my ragged clothes for a page, but they might just believe I really was on an errand.

Into the armoury I marched, letting my eyes search the room, as if seeking someone. Actually, I was soaking in every detail; the walls hung with bright shields and long lances; the tangy smell of metal in the air; the men and boys bustling about, mending bits of armour or polishing them in huge barrels of sand. A massive bellows kept the armoury fire blazing hot, and one man was banging on a strip of heated metal placed on a block. A knight stood in the centre of the room, being measured by the armourer. He caught my gaze and held it.

'What is your business, boy?' he shouted over the din.

I stepped closer, holding out the cloth-covered meat.

'Please sir,' I said, 'Cook told me to bring this leg of pork to one of the knights.'

'Did he! Which one?' The man scowled in disbelief. He had a seamed, sun-browned face with jagged scar running down one side. His piercing eyes looked as though they'd seen plenty of life's troubles.

I swallowed and felt my mouth all dry, but continued as boldly as I could. 'I- I forgot the name, and I didn't like to ask because he would beat me for not listening.' I stood meekly, waiting for the knight to decide what to do, but all the time I was taking in the atmosphere with a throbbing excitement. And here I was, actually talking with a knight!

'Hallo, fellow knights!' the man shouted to the room at large. 'Did one of you order a leg from the kitchen?'

The knights and squires laughed and jeered at this, and a few shouted vulgar remarks.

'No one claims it,' said the knight. His eyes flickered with something like anger. 'Leave it with me; we'll find the man, or make short work of it ourselves.'

I bowed my head humbly and handed over the pork. I was reluctant to go, but I knew I must. At the door, I turned back for one last look, and was unnerved to see the scar-faced knight staring after me.

'Can I try it now?' Odo asked eagerly, when I returned.

'Don't be silly! We'll have to think of something completely different. Nobody would believe two kitchen boys in one day would be sent to the armoury with a leg of pork!'

Odo was completely downcast, so to make up for it, I told him every detail of the armoury, which I could still see clearly in my mind. I would need to remember the room exactly, for later. Next time, I would not be there merely to look.

The Scar-faced Knight

Two nights later I saw my chance. All around me I heard the gentle snores of kitchen boys, each huddled on his favourite patch of straw. I could see a bit of sky beyond the kitchen door. It was completely dark, which suited my plans.

I crept from the kitchen, careful not to wake Odo. Tonight the last thing I needed was a bouncy companion!

I hoped all the knights and squires slept in their tents in the outer bailey. I reckoned there might be a few servants or pages in the armoury, but surely they were asleep. The darkness made it easy to avoid the castle guards as I stole across the courtyard.

I hesitated for a moment at the door of the armoury. There was a bit of light from the banked fire in the corner, but, anyway, my mind could picture the scene clear as day.

Slowly I moved along the wall on my left. Once my toe touched a cloth-covered leg, and I stopped. I held my breath for a moment, hearing a boy murmur in his sleep.

The boy didn't wake. I let out my breath quietly and kept on.

Finally my foot touched something hard. At last - a barrel full of sand, and it was just where I thought.

I felt all around the outside of the barrel. I had counted on there being a couple of mail vests lying about, waiting to be cleaned. Nothing!

Without expecting much, I stuck my hand into the barrel. Lots of sand, and something made of tiny metal links! I drew it out as quietly as I could and blew gently on it to clean off the sand. It was a shirt of ring-mail, fortunately not a large one.

I slipped off my tunic and tried to pull the heavy mail shirt on over my head. I was surprised at how slippery it was; it kept slithering into odd shapes. Finally I bunched it all up together and managed to poke my head through. Then it was easy enough to fit the rest over my body. I replaced my tunic, hoping the metal wouldn't show anywhere. Loose sand got inside my undershirt and began to itch, but I'd have to put up with it for a few days.

I would have kept exploring, but I heard voices outside. Quick as I could I tiptoed to the door and slipped out into the dark yard.

Only a few steps from the armoury I collided with someone.

'Oof!' said a man's voice.

'Beg pardon,' I murmured, jumping backwards, but the person grabbed my tunic. The clouds parted and a glimmer of moonlight shone through. My heart thumped in my throat as I recognised the scar-faced knight.

'It's the kitchen boy, isn't it?' The man held fast to my tunic. Would he feel the mail shirt underneath?

'What are you doing, prowling about?' The man spoke severely.

'Nothing, sir; just getting some air. I was just going back to the kitchen.'

'Wait a moment; I'd have a word with you. What is your name, boy?'

'Uh - John,' I replied, giving the first name I could think of.

'All right, John,' the knight said, in a less harsh tone, 'I am Decourcy. Come aside with me for a moment.'

Decourcy led me to a bench outside the door of the Great Hall. I was filled with a mixture of curiosity and dread, wondering what this knight could want with me.

As soon as we sat down, Decourcy said, 'You made all that up, didn't you, about the leg of pork.'

I nodded miserably.

'And why, pray tell?'

I hesitated; what did I have to lose by telling the truth? The man would surely have me punished, no matter what I said.

'I just wanted to be inside the armoury, to see what it was like.'

Decourcy sighed. 'You think it's one great adventure after another, being a knight.'

I nodded but Decourcy went on.

'Ah yes: adventure, romance - what does a kitchen boy want with all that? You're better off peeling onions your whole life long, I can tell you!' The knight's voice was bitter, and he reached up his hand and stroked his scar with one finger.

There was something about this man that made me sorry for him, and made me bold.

'I've always wanted to be a knight,' I blurted.

'Ever since I can remember, since I knew what knights were, I wanted to be one.' Then I sat still, breathing hard and blushing. Whatever had possessed me to tell this to a stranger?

Decourcy turned towards me. Moonlight made the crevices in his face look like deep rivers. It was an ugly face.

'You remind me of someone I once knew,' Decourcy said. Then he gave a short laugh and added, 'Myself! You even have a scar like mine.'

I put my hand to my cheek; I had forgotten the scar from John's belt, which was healed over.

'You remind me of the boy I was,' the knight went on. 'Wanting to be a knight, looking forward to a life of danger and noble deeds.

'But it's not always like that.' Decourcy stood with a jerky movement. 'Go back to your kitchen, John, and stay there! Be content with what you have.'

He spat this out fiercely, then turned on his heel and stalked across the courtyard. I sat on the bench, watching the knight's stocky figure disappear into the darkness.

What was that all about? The knight's mood settled on me, casting a pall of gloom for which I had no explanation. I went back to the kitchen and threw myself down on my patch of straw, feeling close to despair.

That night, I dreamed I ran through a sunlit forest, chasing a steed the colour of a white stone in moonlight. The horse flitted in and out among the trees, teasing me to follow. The white horse vanished from view. I ran after it, and came upon a grassy meadow, saw a flash of white.

'Wait up!' I called joyfully as I ran forward.

Then I stopped. How could I have thought it was the white horse? It was a large fluffy lamb, like the one in the picture on the church wall in Tenham, and beside it stood a boy, wearing a dirty red tunic.

As I drew closer, I saw with horror that the boy was beating the lamb with a stick. Up and down the stick lashed, until the blood flowed. The lamb was bleating weakly, but still the boy kept on.

'You there!' I shouted, 'stop that!'

The boy raised his head briefly, but then bent it and went on hitting the lamb as before. The boy was just my size and build, and with the same dark, curly hair. The lamb's blood gushed out upon the green grass. I tried to run; I wanted to wrench the stick from the boy's hand and beat him with it, but my body was heavy with dream heaviness. I could not move. I felt sorrow and dread rise within me.

In my dream I began to cry. I cried for the senseless cruelty that made the boy beat the lamb. I cried because I had no power to make the boy stop, and because so much was wrong in life, and no one could make it right.

Then I saw I was astride the white horse and it carried me swiftly onward, until we came to another meadow. A shaft of sunlight flecked the grass with gold, and I saw someone standing in its glow.

It was a young man in a tunic of snowy white, standing tall and straight with a glad smile. Beside him frisked a lamb, whole in every way except for some healed-over scars. Was this the same boy I'd just seen beating the lamb?

'Corin!'

Someone was shaking me roughly, but I tried to clutch onto my dream. It was so beautiful now, and I had to find out who the boy in white was, and why the lamb was well.

'Corin! Wake up.'

'Mmugh,' I answered reluctantly. The dream vanished. My face felt wet. Odo was standing over me with a mug and a hunk of bread.

A Surprise for Robert

The tournament was only one day away. In the kitchen, urchins shoved each other in their haste to prepare for tomorrow's feast, which would end the day. Nearly everything was being cooked ahead, so that even the lowest kitchen boys could watch the jousting. I was grinding cloves with mortar and pestle, aching to sneak off to the armoury.

Lost in a dream world, I saw myself as a squire on the eve of his knighthood. Robed in white, I would kneel before the chapel altar all night. At dawn, I would be bathed and clothed in battle dress, before the knighting ceremony. What coat-of-arms would decorate the tunic and shield of the new Sir Corin?

'Boy!' A box on the ear brought me quickly back to the scene of pungent herbs and sizzling meat. 'Go to the poultry yard and bring back two geese!' Cook ordered.

I slipped thankfully away. If I was quick about it, I could go a roundabout way by the armoury, with no-one the wiser.

Crowds of people were milling about; the castle was bursting at the seams with lords and ladies who had come a long way to see the tournament. I caught a few snatches of conversation, but scarcely noticed. In my mind I was going over my plan for a second night-time foray to the armoury. Tonight was my last chance.

'I must stay awake all night in the chapel, praying,' I overheard a haughty, nasal male voice say, as I neared the armoury.

'I will pray for you, as well, that God may help you in your new duties as a knight.' This was from a girl's voice.

I froze and the hair stood up on my neck. The couple were strolling just in front of me. Lucy and Robert!

'Thank you, Mistress,' Robert replied. 'I pledge myself to honour and protect you, especially after we are wed. And as for your part, of course I expect that you will obey me in all things, without question.'

Lucy murmured a reply that I didn't hear because the blood was rushing noisily to my head. I stood where I was, willing them not to turn around. What were they doing here? And how would that change what I planned for the tournament? They walked on without seeing me.

Robert's arrogant manner made me gnash my teeth. Of course a wife must obey her husband, but I wanted to give the fellow a good thrashing! I was powerless to help Lucy escape from marrying him. For a moment I had a vision of a church door rescue, such as Odo had done for me, but I had to smile at it. By the time I was a knight and had a horse, she'd be long married and probably have a nursery full of children.

I peered in the door of the armoury, and the scene was just as I'd imagined. Young squires were busy readying every piece of equipment for their knights, most of whom were there shouting orders. The air was filled with the sounds of raised male voices, and the clink of steel on steel.

With a sigh, I felt for my own weapon, the dagger which I always wore under my tunic, over the shirt of mail. Would I ever wear more than that one concealed dagger?

'Guess who's come for the tournament,' I whispered to Odo later, as we peeled onions side by side.

'Who?'

'Lucy and Robert!'

Odo turned even more pale than usual. His hair had grown since we'd come, and now a band of orange showed beneath the walnut dye.

'They might recognise us!'

'I don't think so, not if we keep putting dye on your hair. No one notices what servants look like.'

'Anyone else from Tenham?'

'I don't know. I hope Hamo's not still here.'

Odo shook his head gloomily. 'I think we should go back home.'

'Back home!' I exclaimed.

'Well - ' Odo looked down. 'The truth is, this isn't as much fun as I thought it would be. And I miss my family.' I noticed his eyes were damp; maybe it was the onions.

I thought of the family Odo had left behind, his mother and father and four brothers all working together to keep the smithy going. They had the most important task in the village. And it was true, our adventures hadn't come to much.

'You should feel free to go back,' I said, more casually than I felt. It was only fair to let him go if he wanted. 'Your father can keep them from punishing you. But I can't go back. For one thing, the bailiff is out to get me. He's already tried to kill me once! I've got to see if I can make it on my own.'

It was time Odo knew the truth. I was sure now he wouldn't taunt me.

'You know all that business about 'Sir Corin,'' I went on.

Odo nodded.

'Well, it was no jest. Being a knight is something I've always wanted, and I could do it, if someone would take me on and train me. I know I could! I've got an idea about the tournament, a way I could get someone to notice me. And I'm going to go on looking for my father.'

I leaned on a bag of onions and put my chin in my hands. Odo's eyes were bulging. That was when I realised I had said more than I intended.

'Your father?' Odo asked. 'John is in Tenham, you know!'

'John isn't my father,' I said simply, 'and Edith isn't my mother. My mother was a noblewoman, who died when I was born. I'm not sure who my father is.' At least, I hope I'm not sure, I thought.

For the first time in ages my mind turned to John and Edith and Amice, to our tiny cottage, and a wave of feeling washed over me. Could it be that I missed that place, which I was so eager to leave? The memory of the harsh drudgery had dimmed, and all I could think of was Amice, looking at me with adoration, and my snug place in the loft.

Odo ran his hands through his hair, leaving bits of onion skin everywhere.

'So the bundle is something to do with that!' he said finally.

I nodded. I had found a safe hiding place for it under a loose stone in a corner of the kitchen.

'A silver goblet and a book, left by the noblewoman. My mother - Edith - gave them to me. I was born in their cottage and they raised me as their own, but I am not, and somehow, I think I always knew it.'

'Why didn't you tell me sooner?' Odo asked. 'This is more like it! A real adventure - I won't leave you, at least not yet. I'll help you; just tell me what you need!'

Cook was glaring at us, so I whispered, 'Later!' and turned back to my onions, but with a lighter heart.

That night there were two kitchen boys stealing across the courtyard to the armoury. Now that he knew the plan, Odo wouldn't be left behind for anything. I worried that Odo didn't know his way around in the armoury and he'd be sure to crash into something, but there was no stopping him.

The night was not as dark as before. A chilly wind was blowing, and every so often the clouds parted. We ducked down by the wall of the main castle building each time a bit of moonlight shone through. We could hear watchmen on the towers calling out soft jests to each other.

At last we were inside the armoury. I heard Odo's heavy wheezing beside me; just the noise of his breathing would wake the dead! But no one stirred.

I gave him a gentle nudge and he moved off to the right. I skirted around to the left, feeling all around me to see what I could pick up. My foot caught on cloth and I didn't dare to move an inch. What if the person awoke?

Then I realised it was no sleeping form, only folded stuff. I reached down and patted around the folds. There seemed to be a lot of material - more than just a shirt or surcoat. I gathered it up into my arms. Whatever it was, I could use it.

Just about here, I thought, I'd seen some double-bladed swords hanging on the wall. I began to run my hands along the smooth stone until I felt the shock of cold steel. Carefully, quietly, I lifted down the sword from its hook. It was unsheathed, so I wrapped the cloth around it to protect myself from the blade.

'Psst!'

The sound cut the silence like a knife, and I tensed. Couldn't the fellow be quiet? I tiptoed back to the doorway and bumped into Odo.

'I got it!' came the gleeful whisper.

I didn't reply but grabbed my friend's shoulder and jerked him outside.

'Don't you want to see it?' Odo whispered.

'Can't you shut up?' I whispered back fiercely.

'What's going on down there!'

It was a guard on the nearest tower. We froze. The moon was hidden and the man couldn't possibly see us, but that could change at any moment.

'The chapel!' I whispered.

Just a few steps away in the courtyard stood a small chapel. We ducked inside the doorway, huddling together. Odo was holding something large and oddly shaped. Bits of it were poking into my side.

Would the guard come down from his tower to investigate the noise? We waited for what seemed like hours, but nothing else happened. Maybe he thought he'd imagined the noise, or he was just too lazy to bother coming all the way down the winding stairs.

Just when we were standing up and stretching our stiff muscles, the moon peeked out from the clouds. Odo's hand gripped my arm tightly. I looked behind us, where he was pointing.

At the far end of the room was an altar raised up on two stone steps. Someone was lying there on the steps! The moonlight coming in through the window reflected on blond hair.

'Robert!' whispered Odo softly.

Of course! Robert would be knighted tomorrow, before the tournament. He would spend the whole night in prayer, to prepare himself. He must have been deep in prayer, not to hear us come in.

Or was he? 'I think he's asleep!' I murmured.

Odo nodded and chuckled.

'A fine knight! Can't even stay awake one night,' he whispered.

We laid aside what we'd stolen. I now saw that Odo's bulky object was a metal helmet with a huge white wooden swan attached to the top. We crept towards the altar. Sure enough, as we approached, we heard the sound of gentle snoring.

Both of us covered our mouths to stifle the giggles.

I'd like to take the conceited Robert down a peg! I thought. Then I remembered the sharp dagger I carried at my side. A wicked idea crossed my mind.

I reached under my tunic and drew out the dagger. Odo's eyebrows shot up, but he was grinning. We stole nearer and I lifted a lock of Robert's long neatly-curled hair. Now that Odo saw what was happening, he helped by grasping the lock tightly in his fingers, so that Robert wouldn't feel his hair being pulled.

It didn't take long to cut the lock of hair in two. I held it up and we grinned at each other in triumph. After a moment's thought, I laid the lock of blond hair carefully on the step next to Robert's face, where he would be sure to see it in the morning. There would be more than one surprise for Robert tomorrow!

The Tournament

The day dawned crisp and bright. In the field of the outer bailey, colourful pennants fluttered gaily in a light breeze. Crowds lined the arena on every side, and the noise of excited chatter rose on the clear air.

Nobles sat in covered pavilions along the middle of the course, their silks and satins reflecting the sun. Odo and I were crammed together with the poorer folk, who stood behind wooden barriers at the ends.

At last the trumpets sounded, and the crowd roared. A herald stood in the centre of the jousting field, shouting at the top of his lungs. Gradually the hubbub of voices died down.

'The gracious Queen of Love and Beauty,' the herald announced, 'is Mistress Lucy, fair daughter of our honoured guest, Sir Henry. She will award the prizes to the winners.' Applause and deafening cheers from the crowd.

So Sir Henry was here. Well, I expected that. My eyes surveyed the crowds and every so often I saw someone with silver hair, but no bailiff. That was the one person I feared today. He would know me in an instant. Then it would be off to prison - or worse.

I patted the deerskin packet which rested inside my tunic, over the ring-mail shirt. I had it with me today for safekeeping, since I didn't know how the day would turn out.

But I was ready! Last night I had ripped the swan crest from the helmet and cast it into the kitchen fire, over Odo's protests. Odo was carrying the helmet, which now looked like a metal bucket, wrapped in cloth under his arm. I held the stolen sword, wound up in the black cloak I had picked up in the armoury.

Two mounted knights, one in white surcoat and the other in blue, waited at opposite ends of the field. Trumpets sounded; both knights spurred their steeds energetically. The long wooden lances were braced and aimed at each other's chests as they thundered down the course.

WHACK! The noise of impact was like thunder. At first I couldn't sort out what had happened. Then I saw that the blue knight's lance had shattered on the other's shield. Both were still mounted. The blue knight's squire ran out onto the field with a fresh lance.

The young knights made ready and charged again. WHACK! The white knight's lance pierced the wooden crest on the blue's helmet. The crowd cheered wildly, and I saw Lucy at the centre of the stands, waving a bright blue scarf.

On the last charge, both lances shattered with a sharp crack, but the knights just managed to keep their seats. I knew that the weapons were all blunted for safety. If this had been a real battle, one would have been killed by now.

Both knights dismounted and began slashing away with their swords, to the oohs and aahs of the crowd.

The blue knight was down! Groans of disappointment mingled with happy cheers. This joust was over. The loser staggered to his feet, and both knights removed their helmets to bow to their family and friends at the centre stands.

I looked down the field. At the opposite end waited a knight in red on an impressive chestnut charger. A golden bird on his helmet reflected the sun. I knew him instantly by the horse. It was Robert.

'Robert, son of Gregory of Monfort, against Simon, son of John Raymond!' the herald cried.

'Now!' I exclaimed in Odo's ear. 'Hurry!'

At the near end a knight in black was being hoisted up onto a black steed. I darted forward, unwrapping the sword as I went. With my free hand I unfurled the black cloak over my shoulders.

'Wait!' Odo cried. I stopped just long enough for Odo to shove the helmet onto my head and tie the cloak at my neck. Then we ran together into the field.

Two squires were helping the knight mount. Another stood by, holding his long wooden lance. They hadn't seen us running up behind them.

I dashed forward and pushed the knight aside. Odo grabbed the man's helmet and shoved him to the ground. Gasps and shouts went up from the crowd.

The squires were too startled to react, and I swung into the saddle. I kicked the horse's ribs with my bare heels and the beast shied and trotted forward.

'Woo-ha!' I shouted, waving the sword. Probably no one heard me; it was like yelling into a bucket. The helmet made a metallic taste in my mouth. I heard some startled laughter from the peasant sections at the sight of one of their own, barefoot, charging down the field like a drunken knight.

Robert hesitated for a moment, then steadied his lance against his side and spurred his horse sharply. I couldn't see his face for the helmet, but I was sure he was furious.

'Go on; go on!' I shouted, gouging hard with my heels. The horse moved into full gallop. I waved the heavy sword as best I could with one hand and clutched the reins tightly with the other. My body jolted up and down with each step of the horse, nearly flinging me off. It wasn't as easy as I'd thought! I pressed my knees tightly against the animal's sides, and that seemed to help.

Our two horses were rushing for each other at an incredible speed. This was it! This was being a real knight! At the last minute it occurred to me that my own sword wasn't blunted, and that I had no shield to protect myself from Robert's lance.

The slit in my helmet was so small I could barely see, so it wasn't clear what happened next. I felt a jarring crash and something knocked me sideways; the sword was wrenched from my grip and sailed through the air. I hauled myself back into the saddle as the horse slowed to a trot.

When I looked behind me I saw Robert lying flat on his back in the dirt, his wooden lance beside him, severed in two by my sword. At least I didn't kill him! I thought with relief.

The nobles in the stands were stunned into silence, but the peasants and townspeople gave a cheer of appreciation, which dwindled into laughter and excited questioning about my identity. This was just how I'd imagined it! Now they would notice me; they'd see I could do it. Some knight would surely want to take me on!

I laughed, flung off my helmet and waved at the crowd, and the cheer rose again. I caught sight of Lucy in the central pavilion. She wasn't cheering. Her mouth was so far open it looked like her chin would hit her chest.

Someone yanked at my leg and pulled me roughly from the horse. Before I knew it, I was down in the dirt, just like Robert. The crowd switched to jeering and catcalls. I looked up into the face of a man with silver hair. Hamo!

Another man jerked me to my feet. 'Corin, son of John the Red of Tenham,' he said sternly, 'you are under arrest.'

It was over. This must be the sheriff of Ludlow, a burly fellow who was nodding at his men. Two of them seized me and poked and prodded until one exclaimed, 'What's this?' He snatched at the bulge in my tunic, and plucked out the bundle.

'It's mine!' I shouted. I kicked and struggled but the men gripped my arms tightly.

'That belongs to me!' Hamo exclaimed. 'The little devil stole it from my chamber.' He reached out and took the deerskin packet holding the silver goblet and book which might contain the only proof of my parentage. He probably wanted to destroy any evidence of who I was. It was another hint that he really might be my father. I felt my whole being curl up with disgust against him, and I looked away.

'We'll keep him locked up tonight,' the sheriff told Hamo. 'You can take him back to Tenham with you and try him in the manor court. If you think it's a case for the king's court, you'll have to send him back to us.'

The bailiff nodded grimly and clutched the bundle under his arm, as the men led me away.

They marched me across the tournament grounds. I caught sight of Meg in the crowd, looking bewildered. The knight Decourcy stood next to her, saying something in her ear. Odo was nowhere in sight.

In one last glimpse of the scene I saw Robert, his helmet off, bowing to the stands. A few nobles clapped half-heartedly. I noticed with satisfaction that his blond hair was tied back with a cord, to disguise the missing lock.

At the town prison they took my cloak, the shirt of ring-mail and the dagger. All I was left with was undershirt, tunic and torn hose. My legs were clamped in irons and chained to the floor.

The place was crowded with prisoners. A foul smell nearly overpowered me, and the stone floor I sat on was damp. I hoped it was only water. Hands flitted over my body, poking in my tunic.

'Stop that!' I protested.

There was no reply except hoarse chuckles from the two men chained on either side. Maybe they thought I had food. I wished I did; I was starving, and not likely to get any food unless Odo thought to bring some. For his sake, I hoped Odo had headed home to Tenham. I almost smiled at the thought of his mother's face, when she first caught sight of her son's hair!

Then misery descended upon me. All my plans had come to nothing. I would be hauled back to Tenham in disgrace, and at the least, be locked up for a long time. They might even cut my hand off, as a warning to other thieves. 'Sir Corin the Brave' - Corin the Coward was more like it.

With a sudden sharp pang I knew I had been fooling myself, with my high-blown thoughts of knighthood. Peasant boys did not turn into knights. I might as well face it, once and for all.

The whole quest was a silly idea. If Hamo isn't my real father, I thought, I never will find him. Whatever made me think I could just wander about in the world, and stumble across that one person? And even if I did find him, I have no proof. Hamo has taken it.

I shuddered with revulsion against this evil man. I couldn't avoid the possibility that I had found my real father, that the bailiff was the very man I sought. What would that mean for me, Corin? Was a son doomed to become like the father? Would something begin to sour and rot within me, until I was like Wat, a perfect mirror of cruelty?

Yes, it had already begun! Vivid pictures of my own wrongs swam before my eyes. I lied whenever I wanted my own way; I had betrayed my loyalty to my mother and to Lucy, by running off. I'd stolen the coins and dagger and now the armour.

'But I had to do all those things!' I muttered aloud.

Ah yes, my heart accused me, you had to do them because you think of no one but yourself! You are as full of selfishness as a pudding is of raisins! You call Hamo evil; how are you different?

A terrible knowledge swept over me. It took my breath away. I was the boy in red beating the lamb in the meadow, in my last dream. My wrongdoings were like the blows wounding the lamb.

'No!' I began to sob, hardly hearing the scornful sniggers from the darkness. 'I don't want it to be true! I don't want to be cruel and evil. O Holy Mother - ' I began to pray, in spite of the mocking laughs of the men. Then I stopped. I could no longer picture the wooden statue to which I once told my troubles.

I thought instead of the painting on the church wall in Tenham, showing the Lord Christ as a pierced lamb who didn't seem to notice his own wounds. Suddenly I understood for the first time what that meant. The Lord Jesus had been hung up on a cross and left to die a horrible death. But He was willing for it to happen. He let himself be slaughtered like a sacrificial lamb. Why? Why would anyone willingly go through torture and death?

Some words came into my mind, words spoken by the Lollard preacher, Stephen's friend. 'Christ paid the price for your sins, when he died on the cross.' Was that it? Was the Lord Christ willing to die a painful death, to pay for my selfishness?

I thought of the wounded lamb in the meadow, in my dream. I put my head between my knees, so I wouldn't be heard. 'Christ, the Lamb of God,' I whispered.

159

I knew I wasn't good, could never be, on my own. I didn't deserve Heaven! But I began to be aware that I didn't need to, if only I could get the Lord Christ to forgive me. Stephen had said I could speak my heart directly to Him, so I pushed my head further between my knees and began.

'I don't want to be cruel,' I whispered. 'I'm sorry for everything - most of all that I seem to be completely selfish.'

I thought again of the dream. Then I knew I was not just the boy in red, lashing out at the lamb in the meadow. I was the other boy as well, the one who stood clothed in white, with the healed lamb frisking at my side.

'I want you to forgive me,' I whispered. 'I open my heart to you. I want to be that boy in white.'

All around me I could hear moans and curses, and squeaks from the rats. This was the most wretched place I had ever been. I covered my nose with my hands, trying to muffle the stench. What would tomorrow bring? What harrowing turn would my life take next?

On Trial

Two days later I stood, hands bound behind my back, in the Great Hall of Tenham manor. It had been two days of shame and misery and uncertainty. I did not know if I was forgiven, any more than I knew what the future would hold.

Sir Henry sat at the centre of the head table in a massive crimson gown, flanked on either side by his elderly steward, and Master Stephen. On the table in front of Stephen were parchment, quills and ink. Several men from the village sat at either end, and other villagers lined the walls.

Mistress Lucy was seated to one side, and Robert next to her. Robert glowered at me and crossed his arms as if to keep his hands from strangling me. I knew I had ruined the squire's first tournament, so he had a right to be furious. Maybe I should have felt sorry, but I didn't.

A man-at-arms led me up to the front and made me bow to the head table. I avoided looking at Hamo, who sat stiffly at the end.

What would become of me? Fear of the future washed over me. I listened distractedly as the court began.

'John the Red,' called out the steward in a cracked voice, 'come and stand with your son.' John, his face like thunderclouds, stepped up beside me.

Sir Henry opened the session. 'Corin, son of John the Red: you are accused of leaving Tenham village without permission, and of stealing. Master Hamo will explain.' He waved his plump hand in the direction of the bailiff.

'This boy has always been a troublemaker,' began the bailiff, his blue eyes like the ice on a pond. 'Now we finally have proof of his crimes!'

Crimes! My temper flared. If there was crime in Tenham, it was committed by this very man. If only Odo and I had been able to find out exactly what it was! I glanced around for Odo, and caught a glimpse of his freckled face among the villagers standing on the left.

'The boy is a thief!' Hamo pointed his finger dramatically at me.

'The question is,' said Sir Henry, 'what did he steal? If it was anything of value, we'll have to send him to the king's court.'

'Sire, he stole a helmet, mail shirt, sword and cloak from the armoury at Ludlow,' the bailiff replied. I wasn't surprised he didn't mention what was taken from his chest. 'And of course, to the crime of stealing we must add his escape, and his unthinkable act at the tournament.' There was a suppressed growl from Robert.

'Do you have anything to say for yourself?' asked Sir Henry sternly.

I took a gulp of air and tried to give myself confidence by throwing my shoulders back and chin up. As I raised my head, Stephen's gaze met mine. His brown eyes held depths of kindness.

Somehow that look of Stephen's told me what I wanted to know: God had forgiven me! I broke out into a sweat with the relief of it, and nearly smiled. It was like sunlight beaming into one window of a dark dungeon, shining a small shaft of hope into my misery. It was like jumping all hot and dirty into a clear deep pool and feeling layers and layers of grime wash away.

Was this what Stephen meant about being a true Christian? The court might decide to lock me away in prison, but in my heart I was free. They might brand me a criminal, but I felt clean in my deepest self. That was the main thing!

I spoke as loudly as I could.

'Sire, it's true that I escaped and stole the armour.' I knew no one would believe me, but I would tell the truth. 'But Master Hamo also stole something valuable from me. And I think he's been stealing from you as well!'

The bailiff leapt to his feet and his face twitched violently. 'This boy is babbling!' he exclaimed. 'Sire, I appeal to you; you can tell he is not to be trusted.'

But Sir Henry merely folded his hands over his wide stomach, and settled more comfortably into his chair. 'I would hear the boy out,' he said with determination. Then he peered closer at me. 'Isn't this the boy who rescued my wife and daughter from the fire? We seem to see a lot of you these days! Go on, lad.'

'Well, Sire,' said I, 'Odo and I tried to search Master Hamo's chamber.'

'That's right,' Hamo said, 'don't you remember, Sire, I caught them at it! This boy must be punished!'

Henry put up his hand for silence, and nodded at me to continue.

'Before I escaped,' I went on, 'I went back to Master Hamo's room, and found a secret compartment in his chest. The valuables of mine were there, and some bags of gold florins.'

Hamo's dark face drained of colour as he heard this. Wat, who had been standing just behind him, began to slink backwards through the throng. The watchers whispered to one another.

'Sire, if I may, I can add something to this.'

At this the whispers became a chatter of questioning. Who was this stranger? What was this about? I turned my head. Standing at the back of the hall by the entrance, was the scar-faced knight Decourcy.

For a brief moment the bailiff stood transfixed. Suddenly, with a bellow of rage, he thrust his way through the throng and vaulted out one of the tall windows of the Great Hall.

There was an anguished shriek. 'My jewels!' Dame Margaret stood near the window, wailing and wringing her hands. The carved ivory case was nowhere to be seen.

'Catch him!' bawled Sir Henry, struggling to his feet. Decourcy ran outside in pursuit.

Every man present tried to follow, crashing into one another in the confusion. Everyone else crowded to the windows to see what was happening. There were shrieks of 'Head him off! Head him off! Not the church!'

I wanted to see what was happening, but there was no chance of getting near door or window.

Odo scrambled up onto his brother's back.

There was a clatter of hooves and I caught a glimpse of silver hair as Hamo galloped out the gate, clutching the jewel case under one arm.

'He's taken my horse!' Decourcy shouted.

Knights and men-at-arms stumbled over each other in their haste to reach the stables. For a few moments the courtyard looked like a battlefield, but finally several of the men were horsed and thundering after the bailiff. The rest, including Decourcy, returned to the hall.

Sir Henry eased his body wearily into his chair. 'Will someone please tell me what this is about?' he demanded.

In a flash I remembered the muffled cart I had heard going down the street in the middle of a dark night, after the sheepshearing. At the same time I thought of seeing Hamo burning what looked like tally sticks, out behind the manor house. I guessed what must have been in the cart: Sir Henry's wool, stolen by the bailiff, being taken away for sale! And the gold florins hidden in the chest were his payment.

'Sire,' I said boldly, 'I think the bailiff has been stealing wool from the manor.'

Sir Henry's eyes bulged in disbelief, but he listened as I told about hearing the cart on the night of the shearing. I added, 'Sire, it may be that you have a lot more sheep than you think. I believe the bailiff recorded the count as lower than it really was.'

Sir Henry's face went scarlet. 'That means the scoundrel could sell the extra wool on his own, and pocket the money! Why did you not see the flaw?' Sir Henry asked in exasperation, turning to the steward.

'The tallies always seemed right,' the old steward protested in a quavering voice. 'I knew nothing of this.'

'Please, Sire - I saw the bailiff burning sticks once, in the back of the manor garden. He could burn the true tally sticks and mark false ones to keep!'

Sir Henry sat speechless at this. Just then Stephen called out from the back of the Hall, 'We have it, Sire!' I had not noticed him slip out. 'I found the bags of gold coin in the bailiff's chest, just as Corin said. And something else.'

Stephen set my bundle down in front of Sir Henry and unwrapped the leather covering. Oohs and aahs went up from the crowd as Sir Henry held the goblet and book up for all to see. He dumped out the contents of the little leather bag, and gold florins rolled across the table.

'Well!' exclaimed Sir Henry. 'Where did this come from?'

'The book and goblet are mine,' I said.

At this chuckles broke out among the crowd. John glared at me as if he couldn't believe I was so stupid.

'They are yours,' Sir Henry said in a sarcastic tone.

'Yes, Sire. They were given to me.' I was gathering courage, the more I spoke.

'You don't expect us to believe this!' Sir Henry exclaimed.

At that Mistress Lucy stood and came forward, a determined expression on her pale face.

'I don't believe he stole these things, Father. He showed me the book once and asked me to read it for him.' More exclamations from the villagers at this. 'Would he have done that if it were stolen?'

'He is no thief!' A woman's voice rang out from the crowd. Edith, my mother, pushed her way forward. 'Sire, I can explain about the book and goblet. My son is no thief!' Her voice shook.

'Woman, hold your tongue!' John growled.

'I cannot,' she replied with a sob. Her face was white and she looked near fainting.

A murmur of astonishment spread through the assembly. For a wife to defy her husband, and in public! Even more unlikely, that it should be Edith!

'Hold your tongue, I tell you, or be sorry for it!' John hissed these words fiercely through his teeth, and a vein at his temple throbbed violently.

Decourcy shouldered his way to the front and stood next to John.

'I beg your pardon, Sire,' he said, addressing Sir Henry, 'but I may be able to add something to the purpose here.'

The Past Unlocked

'Sire, may I have your leave to tell a story?' asked Decourcy.

Sir Henry nodded, and the knight stepped forward and turned to face the assembly. Although not tall, he was an impressive figure, with his muscular chest and the gash running down the left side of his face. He waited until the noise of questions and exclamations had ceased, and every ear was pricked in anticipation.

Why had Decourcy followed us here? I supposed he would tell how I wanted to be a knight, as evidence there was some good in me. I felt myself blushing furiously; the man would expose my confidences before the whole village!

'I am Decourcy, a distant relation of Baron Mortimer of Ludlow. Fifteen years ago I married a girl from a noble Ludlow family,' Decourcy began.

'She was a lovely creature, and a good wife. But I'm sorry to say I was headstrong and - well, I used to beat her at my whim.' As Decourcy said this, I was astonished to see what looked like a tear in the corner of his eye.

'One night I had drunk too much, and I beat and slapped her even though I knew she was with child. I know it was wrong, and I have sought God's mercy. But I cannot undo what happened. That night she took her old nurse and left in secret, and I have never seen her since.'

The silence that followed this was full of each person's thoughts. I felt the blood pounding in my ears. I held my breath.

Sir Henry broke the silence, in a respectful tone. 'Sir Decourcy, can you explain what bearing this has on our court?'

'Yes I can,' the knight replied. He hesitated briefly, and then went on. 'I told you that my name is Decourcy; that is my family name. What I did not say is that my Christian name is Corin. I want to know the history of this boy who stands accused, and who looks as much like my dear wife as anyone I have met!'

At this the room was in an uproar. Edith burst into tears and was comforted by two village wives. Amice clung to her skirts and wailed.

The rest of those gathered in the Great Hall shouted to one another above the din, many saying that, of course, they knew all along there was something about the lad. Odo wormed his way to my side and grinned as if his freckled face would split.

'It do be a true story,' someone called out.

At first I couldn't see who had said this, but then I gaped in surprise as a squat fellow pushed through the throng. Wat!

The boy grinned at me and spoke in my ear, 'I'm telling your secret, like it or not!' He giggled and turned to address the court.

'My mother, what died last year, told me she

was close to their cottage when he were born,' he said, nodding at me. 'She told me a stranger lady had him!'

He leered triumphantly as he made the announcement. Evidently Wat didn't have enough wit to understand that it was to my advantage.

John stood as if skewered to the floor, opening and closing his mouth. It was clear he did not know whether to be furious or glad, that this matter hidden for nearly fourteen years was revealed. His dark eyes darted from Decourcy to Sir Henry and back. I figured he was waiting to see if the thing could be turned to his benefit. He growled low in his throat when Edith spoke again, but did not try to prevent her.

'Sire,' she said, addressing Decourcy in a soft, sad voice, 'I am sorry to tell you that your wife died in childbirth. It was wrong, I know, but we raised the boy as our own and we - I loved him as my own.' This last she said in a whisper.

Decourcy bowed his head and kept it down so no one could see his face.

My own feelings were muddled. At first I was incredibly happy when I realised that, if Decourcy was my real father, then Hamo could not be. I could have taken anything except that! But this knight was not the father I had dreamed about. He was a knight, to be sure, but he admitted to being cruel, a man who caused the death of his innocent wife - my mother. His stocky figure and seamed, ugly face didn't live up to my idea of what a knight should look like.

'Well!' said Sir Henry, 'I suppose all we need is

some proof that this is all as you say. If Sir Decourcy will tell us whether the book and goblet belonged to his wife....'

Decourcy picked up the silver goblet and ran his sun-browned hand over it. He opened the book and glanced inside. His face lit up briefly as with a happy memory, but then it clouded over.

'Before we married,' he said, 'my wife was lady-in-waiting for a year to our late Queen. Queen Anne was a great one for reading the scriptures, and she gave this to my wife when she left her to marry me and move to Chester. She signed it personally. It was my Rosamund's most treasured possession.'

Sir Henry cleared his throat. 'Then I believe we are all in agreement that the boy should go free,' he said, and the villagers seated at the table nodded.

'Sir Decourcy, if you will, retire with me to the solar, and bring the boy with you. Stephen, you as well!' With a sigh Sir Henry heaved his bulk from the carved chair and lumbered off, with his wife and Robert and Lucy following.

A man-at-arms unlocked my chains and I rubbed my sore wrists. Decourcy looked at me gravely and motioned for me to follow. I went, not trusting myself to glance at John. But as I passed by Edith, the woman I knew as Mother, I touched her arm and she smiled at me through her tears.

Amice was pouting at me but I winked at her and she grinned. This could never change things between us.

I followed the men into the solar, the room with its polished wooden furniture and bright tapestries, and I thought of the time when I had surprised

Lucy on the solar stairs. That seemed years ago, but I felt the same now: I might be the son of a knight, but I looked and smelt like a scruffy peasant boy, and I had no inkling of how to act. I stood as close to Decourcy as I could without actually hiding behind him.

Then I felt a slender hand touch mine.

'I am so glad for this,' said Mistress Lucy softly, ' - Cousin.'

'C-cousin?' I stuttered.

'It's true!' she exclaimed, dissolving into giggles. 'Decourcy is related to the Mortimers, and so are we! I'm sure that makes us some sort of cousin.'

At this Robert sneered and with a murmured 'By your leave, Sire!' left the solar in a huff. I felt myself grinning stupidly.

'My jewels, my jewels,' Dame Margaret moaned softly as she sank into a chair by the fire, clasping and unclasping her hands. She seemed unaware of anything that had happened.

'Sire, if I may speak further,' said Decourcy, when all were seated. My chief concern was what to do with my hands, which seemed huge and awkward. I finally solved the problem by sitting on them.

Sir Henry nodded.

'My liege lord is Baron Gilbert of a manor near Chester.'

'Gilbert - I seem to know a Baron Gilbert. Where have I heard that name before?' muttered Sir Henry.

'Perhaps your bailiff, Hamo, may have mentioned that he came from the manor of Baron Gilbert. I knew him there.'

'Ah yes!' Sir Henry stuck the arm of his chair.

'That was it. He brought a letter from Baron Gilbert, attesting to his faithful service under the baron.'

Decourcy smiled, and his scar crinkled oddly. The smile did not reach his eyes.

'That letter was surely a forgery,' he said. 'Hamo was the baron's nephew and did make himself useful as his steward, but he realised he would never inherit, as the baron has four sons. So one day Hamo simply disappeared. I'm afraid a quantity of gold disappeared with him.'

'By the heavens!' Sir Henry burst out. 'The man was truly a knave!'

'He was. The baron was hurt, but after all, Hamo was his nephew, so he didn't give chase. Hamo probably planned all along to rob from you as much and as long as he could, and then disappear again.

'I think his plans went awry when he met Corin here. He knew my wife and the whole story of how she had left just before her time to give birth. The name, coupled with Corin's resemblance to my dear wife - '

'That's why he acted the way he did!' I spoke before I checked myself, then clamped his lips together in embarrassment.

'Go on,' Stephen urged. 'It's all right; you may speak.' Sir Henry nodded.

'Ever since Master Hamo heard my name, he was after me, and I couldn't think why. I thought - I was afraid - ' But there was no way I was going to admit to what I had feared. Stephen looked at me with a flash of understanding.

'That was it,' Decourcy agreed. 'Perhaps he

guessed the book might help you find me. He must have had a shock when he saw me at Ludlow Castle!'

I worked up my courage to speak again. 'Sire, did - did you know who I was from that first time I came into the armoury?'

Decourcy smiled. 'No, not at all! I only knew there was something familiar about you. And you told me your name was John!' I shook my head at my own stupidity.

'It wasn't until the tournament. After you took off your helmet, I turned and there was old Meg next to me in the crowd. Seeing you both together like that, hearing the Sheriff call your name, I suddenly knew. It was a good thing you did your crazy joust, or this all might be turning out differently!'

'I saw you with Meg,' I said, 'but I don't understand - '

Decourcy grinned. 'So you know Meg! I've brought her to Tenham with me. She was your mother's nurse from childhood.'

I was stunned. The poor woman, driven mad by the death of her mistress. She must have wandered aimlessly all those years. I wondered if she saw in me a resemblance to my dead mother.

'My jewels, my precious jewels!' wailed Dame Margaret, cutting into my thoughts.

'Woman, leave it!' snapped Sir Henry. 'You and Lucy retire now.' Lucy took her mother by the hand and led her out. At the doorway she turned back and smiled at me. Then with a flicker of blue silk, she was gone.

Later that night, I sat with Stephen and Decourcy in the solar. We had gathered our chairs in front of the fireplace, where a cheery blaze kept the chill of the room at bay.

We sat quietly, each gazing into the fire and thinking his own thoughts. In the silence I tried to take in all that had happened that day. In one blow I had been snatched from the door of prison and made son to a knight. It was my quest come true, but I all I could feel now was numbness.

'Corin.' Decourcy spoke in a low, solemn tone.

'Yes, uh - ' I was confused. What should I call this man?

'You may call me 'Decourcy.'' His blue eyes held the hint of a twinkle but he did not smile.

'Yes, Decourcy.' I breathed out with relief. I was not ready to name him Father.

'Corin, I know I did a great wrong to your mother - and to you.' Decourcy sighed and shifted in his chair, staring into the fire. 'For years I have sought God's forgiveness. I even made a pilgrimage to Rome. I knocked at every door where I thought I would find it.'

I sat very still. This sounded very much like what had happened to me!

'I stayed awhile at the abbey in Shrewsbury,' Decourcy went on. 'Finally one of the brothers explained to me that God was offering me forgiveness the whole time, through his Son's death on the cross. All I needed to do was reach out to him, and take the pardon He offered. I was seeking Him, but He found me! That was two years ago; since then, I've been looking for my wife and child, hoping you were still alive.'

I looked across at Stephen and drew courage from the kindness in his face.

'Something like that happened to me,' I said quietly, and both men sat up straighter. 'And I was looking for you. That's one reason I left Tenham in the first place.'

'Well then perhaps - ' Decourcy began, 'I had hoped - perhaps you will be able someday to forgive me. Your life would have been very different if I hadn't been so selfish.'

I did not reply, nor did Decourcy seem to demand an answer. Yes, I wanted to forgive, only everything was too new and I needed time to know what I was feeling about anything.

I began to understand that being a true Christian had something to do with change. Change that began on the inside, invisible, but which would work its way through to the outside, where others could see it. Decourcy must be a very different person now from what he was earlier, when he got drunk and abused my mother.

And even though he had driven her to her death - and made my life less than it could have been - I knew that the Lord Christ was beginning to make changes in me as well, and it wouldn't be long before I would forgive this man, my father.

The three of us sat in comfortable silence, watching the fire die down.

'There's only one thing we have not discussed,' Decourcy said some time later.

'What's that?' I asked.

Decourcy smiled, and for once the smile reached

to his eyes. The long scar was hardly noticeable when he smiled like that.

'It's just that I'm wondering: when do you want to start learning to be a knight?'

At that I could not help myself. I leaped out of my chair and gave a whoop of sheer delight.

Out Into the Sunshine

'Take that! And that, and that!'

'Ow-w! That hurt!' Odo staggered back and clutched his arm.

'Boys, boys - good thing I didn't let you use real swords yet!'

Decourcy stepped between us and pushed us apart. 'Softly! Strike decently and in order.'

'But it's been weeks since we started,' I protested, 'and we're still using wooden swords, like babies!'

Sir Henry had invited us to stay at Tenham Manor until after the feast of St. Martin's, when his family and entourage would move on. I slept in the armoury tower with Decourcy and the other knights and squires.

Decourcy had made me squire, to replace his own recently knighted one, and he let Odo come and practice with me. Not that Odo would ever become a knight. He was happy to stay in Tenham with his family, but Decourcy and I would move on when Sir Henry left. Decourcy planned to take me with him back to Chester, and old Meg as well.

Decourcy's horse had been found quietly grazing in a field near Ludlow three days after the bailiff's escape. I wondered where Hamo was and whether I would ever run across him again.

I had my own horse now! It was only an ordinary grey, but a sturdy animal, and I was learning how to make it know I was its master. I still hoped for a really fine white charger, tall and sleek, the colour of a white stone in moonlight.

'I wish I was going with you after all,' said Odo later that evening, as we sat on a bench along the wall in the Great Hall.

Rain rattled against the shuttered windows, invading the chimney with a few drops which set the fire hissing. Two chairs were pulled close to the fire. Decourcy dozed in one and Meg's bulk filled the other, her head lolling to one side. She was calmer now that Decourcy was here, and she smiled more.

'No you don't,' I said, yanking down on my tight hose. I had finally got used to the sturdy leather boots Decourcy had bought for me, but still would have felt more at home in my old ragged tunic and saggy hose. 'You'd miss your family too much.'

I knew I would miss my family, when it came down to it. I would sorely miss my mother and Amice, and maybe even John. Sir Henry had made him a free man, now that I was discovered to be of noble blood, and John went around these days in a glow.

He'd been furious, though, about the goblet and book. 'Could have bought our freedom several times over!' he had fumed. Maybe he'd wanted to give me a good thrashing over that, but he knew he had no right to. I gave Edith the goblet to remember me by, but I made John promise not to sell it. I grinned as I thought of how he had sputtered over that!

'Maybe I would miss them a little,' Odo admitted. 'But you haven't heard the latest. I now have a reason to leave. Guess who I'm supposed to be betrothed to.'

'Not Muriel!'

Odo nodded and made a woeful face. 'It's all Stephen's fault. He's convinced I should marry Muriel, just because he feels sorry for her!'

'Well, you don't seem over worried,' I observed. 'Have you taken to liking her?'

Odo grabbed me by the throat and pulled me to the floor, and we rolled around yelling and laughing.

'Stop it, you two! What are you doing?'

We sat up and saw Mistress Lucy glaring down at us with hands on hips, but the corners of her mouth were twitching.

'All right,' she said, 'I want to know all about it.'

Odo and I followed her back to the bench. Lucy had discovered she was six months older than me, and had taken to mothering me. I wasn't sure I liked it. She clucked in sympathy when she heard us out.

'Poor Muriel!'

'Poor Muriel?' Odo said.

'Yes, she's had an awful time, if you think about it. Maybe I'll ask Father if I can have her to be my maid. I haven't really wanted a maid, but it might be a good thing for her.

'As far as being married goes, you can get out of it if you try hard enough,' she went on. 'I had to bother Father about Robert until he was thoroughly put out, but he finally said I didn't have to marry him. Anyhow, I don't think Robert was so keen any more, thanks to Corin! Luckily we weren't officially betrothed yet. Now Mother is worried that I'll be a spinster, just because I'm nearly fourteen and not yet promised to anyone!

'At least it's taken her mind off the jewels, poor thing,' Lucy went on. 'With the bailiff not yet found, I'm sure her jewels are gone for good. There were so many special things, handed down for ever so long.'

At that moment Stephen came bounding into the hall, drenched with rain. He was followed almost on his heels by Wat, who had been declared too simple-minded to be punished for anything he might have helped the bailiff do.

Now that the bailiff had left, Stephen had taken Wat under his wing and was trying to reform him into something more human. I thought privately that it was effort wasted, but then you never knew. Stephen was so full of the love of God, maybe some of it would spill over onto Wat.

'Time for our English lesson,' Stephen said, and we made room for him on the bench. He dried his hands carefully on the underside of his tunic, and reached inside the leather scrip that hung from his belt.

He pulled out a leather-wrapped bundle, untied the thongs, and lifted something out. It was my book. Stephen gazed reverently at it for a moment, then eased his hands between the gold-leaved pages and opened it at the middle. I smiled as I remembered Stephen's face when he had first looked inside it and found it was the four gospels, written in the English tongue.

It was not long afterwards that he had begun to teach me to read the symbols stretched across the parchment pages, and I enjoyed seeing words come alive almost as much as I did learning sword skills from Decourcy.

I never lost the feeling of awe at seeing the row upon row of neat brown letters, handwritten by some monk who spent his whole life in the making of books. The coloured borders winked in the firelight, intricate designs in gold and red and blue.

Stephen began to read aloud the English words, and my mind wandered. These months had brought unbelievable change in the life of a villein boy. I was turned in an instant from peasant to noble, and my life would never be the same. Stephen said that was a picture of what had happened when I opened my heart to the Lord Christ: in that instant I had become part of a family of true believers, who were Christians not because they lived in a Christian land, but because Christ's forgiveness was real in their lives. It was like living your whole life locked away in prison and then suddenly being let out into the sunshine, free.

I glanced over at Decourcy as he dozed by the fire, and felt a warm glow for him fill my heart. In these past weeks I'd been asking the Lord Jesus Christ to help me forgive this man. In that moment I knew that it had happened, and my prayer was answered.

What lay ahead? The years of training as squire, perhaps even in real combat. Finally that glorious day, when after my all-night vigil in the chapel, I would be made a knight. And then what? The quest had also led me to my father, and to forgiveness, yet my life did not end here. There would be other things I would need as I grew older. I knew I was still very selfish, but maybe now that I was a true Christian I would begin to change little by little, until someday I might love others the way Stephen did, like a fire which warmed the house.

The path of my future seemed to lie clear and straight before me. I knew there would be other times when I would have to ask and seek and knock. But I was sure the right way would open before me, if I sought it with my whole heart.

Ten Things to Know
About Life in the Middle Ages

1 *Who were the 'Haves' and the 'Have-nots' in the medieval village?*

The 'lord' of the farming estate lived in the manor house, sometimes owning several houses and moving around as supplies ran low. Peasants, also called 'serfs' or 'villeins' either paid rent to farm strips of land, or else gave a portion of their produce to the lord. He owned them and all their possessions. If a villein could escape and was not caught in a year and a day, he would be free.

2 *Why were walls built around towns?*

A castle and the surrounding town were built closely together and walled for defense.

'Town air makes men free' was a saying, although in fact the air was probably not very fresh! The townspeople paid taxes to the king instead of being owned by a manor lord. Towns were exciting, lively places, but at high risk of fire or disease due to overcrowding.

3 How were criminals punished?

A thief might have a hand cut off, slanderers could have their ears cropped, rowdiness could be punished by being chained with head and hands in a pillory. Suspected witches were thrown into a pool; if they sank, they were innocent (though dead!) but if they floated, they were guilty and were burned at the stake. Hanging was common not only for murder but also for rioting and serious robbery.

4 How did men become knights?

At age 14, a boy of noble class who had served as a page might be made a squire, the personal servant to a knight. He would spend four years getting used to wearing heavy armour and training with horse, sword and lance. At age

18 after a night alone in prayer he could be knighted, promising to defend churches, orphans, widows and all the servants of God.

5 What was battle like?

The goal was to stay as far from the enemy as possible. Bows and arrows or spears were used first, and archers carried a 'meat-cleaver' sword, sharp on one edge only, to use as a last resort. Two-edged swords were for close fighting wearing armour, and required much training. It took a half an hour to suit up a knight in full gear. If a suit of armour fit well, a knight could take a bad fall from a horse, get up, shake his metal joints loose and walk away.

6 What caused the 'Black Death' plague?

Rats carrying fleas which host the plague bacillus spread the plague all over Europe in the mid-1300's. Whole villages were wiped out and a third of the population of England died. Symptoms included egg-sized boils, coughing

and fever. Some people thought it was caused by God's anger; others that it was an evil mist rising from a strange coinciding of the planets.

7 How was the church central to daily life?

The clergy had great authority in Western Europe in the Middle Ages. Most people thought of themselves as Christians and would donate money to build vast stone cathedrals in each town. These often took a hundred years to complete, and would hold all the inhabitants of a community of five thousand.

8 Why was going on pilgrimage so popular?

People would travel to shrines which held a bit of bone or other 'relic' of a dead saint, hoping for forgiveness from a sin, or  to be healed. The most popular places were Rome, Santiago de Compostela in northern Spain, Canterbury in England and of course, Jerusalem. Each shrine had its own small lead badge, which pilgrims would sew on their hats to show where they had been.

9 Who first translated the Bible into English?

 John Wycliffe was a professor at Oxford University in the fourteenth century. He was constantly in trouble for speaking out against the wrongs of the church. He encouraged the translation of the Bible from Latin into English, so that people could read it for

themselves. His followers were travelling friars called 'Lollards', who were persecuted for spreading his ideas. Today there are still 380 million people in the world who have no Bible in their native language.

10 How did the English language develop?

When the Anglo-Saxons conquered Britain in the sixth century AD they brought their Germanic language, which we now call 'Old English'. Then the Norman French came in the eleventh century, so the ruling class spoke French. These two languages combined over the years, helped by the popular writer Geoffrey Chaucer who wrote 'The Canterbury Tales' in what we know as 'Middle English'. This was the forerunner of modern English and would have been the language spoken by Corin in the late fourteenth century.

If you enjoyed this book
look out for our other title
in the series

TALES · OUT · OF · TIME

KING ARTHUR'S
Ransom
DONNA VANN

Time Period: Dark Ages

Torchbearers
Danger On The Hill

by C. Mackenzie

"Run, run for your lives," a young boy screamed.
"Run, everybody, run. The soldiers are here."

That day on the hill is the beginning of a new
and terrifying life for the three Wilson children.
Margaret, Agnes and Thomas are not afraid to stand
up for what they believe in, but it means that they
are forced to leave their home and their parents for
a life of hiding on the hills.

If you were a covenanter in the 1600s you were
the enemy of the King and the authorities. But all
you really wanted to do was worship God in the
way he told you to in the Bible. Margaret wants to
give Jesus Christ the most important place in her
life, and this conviction might cost her life.

*There is danger on the hill for Margaret. There
is danger everywhere - if you are a covenanter.*

The Torchbearers series are true life stories from
history where Christians have suffered and died
for their faith in Christ.

ISBN 1 85792 7842

CHRISTIAN FOCUS

Staying faithful – Reaching out!

Christian Focus Publications publishes books for adults and children under its three main imprints: Christian Focus, Mentor and Christian Heritage. Our books reflect that God's word is reliable and Jesus is the way to know him, and live forever with him.

Our children's publication list includes a Sunday school curriculum that covers pre-school to early teens; puzzle and activity books. We also publish personal and family devotional titles, biographies and inspirational stories that children will love.

If you are looking for quality Bible teaching for children then we have an excellent range of Bible story and age specific theological books.

From pre-school to teenage fiction, we have it covered!

Find us at our web page:
www.christianfocus.com